Karma's Curse

A novel

by

Takeshia McIntyre

Published by
TruthWriterMcIntyre
207 South 16th Street
Wilmington, NC 28401

Copyright © 2018
Takeshia McIntyre

ISBN 978-1-7335135-0-0

Edited by John H. Meyer
Cover design by Kathleen Beall Meyer
~ www.CapeFearPublishers.com ~
Cover illustration by Damali Vallier

Publisher's Note
This book is a work of fiction. The names, characters, places and
incidents are the product of the author's imagination. Any similarity
to actual persons, living or dead, business establishments, events or
locales is entirely coincidental.

Chapter 1
The difference between life and death

I took my first step in learning how to kill when I was six years old.

That step was to understand the difference between life and death. I had to understand that once you take a life, there's no way to bring it back. So when I make the decision to kill, I was taught, I have to make sure I have a complete reason to do so.

"You must not make any mistakes with killing," Daddy told me. "In time you will understand my reasons for saying so. The materials I'm going to provide for you from now on are all lethal weapons. For killing purposes only." He spoke to me like he was making a speech. When he finally finished, it was time to go to the quiet room and start training.

~

My name is Karma and I'm a serial killer. You see, my father trained me to become a professional assassin. I didn't want this life but I basically was born to kill.

I'm not proud of my murders I committed but I'm not ashamed, either. I don't even regret what I have done. All I know is that now it's getting the best of me. The murders are starting to become a necessity and I don't know how to let go. Through my twenty-five years I've already killed over fifty people. After the tenth one, I just stopped counting. During my journey through life I've also blackmailed and robbed people to become what I am now. I've killed preachers, judges and boyfriends. All of them deserved it, of course. At least I thought they did. I know you're probably judging me already; but you don't know my story. The only way you might understand me is if you hear this.

Honestly, I hope you understand. But I know I have a problem. Maybe, hopefully, you can help me solve it. I know you're saying, "Why would I want to help you after all that has happened?" But you must know that everything is not what it seems. I need you to try to walk a day in my shoes and see where you end up.

~

When Daddy started my training, he had me wearing size 12 running shoes. Before long, I was running three miles a day and swimming a mile a day. It was fun to me. I enjoyed training; every minute of it. My father showed me how to take guns apart, handle and shoot them correctly. Other girls my age were playing with their Barbies and Beanie Babies; the toys I loved were my guns. At the age of six, I had four but they were only nine millimeters.

Monday through Friday, from 5:30 in the morning to 1:00, I was running, swimming, boxing, and learning ninja moves. I was also learning the silent ways to kill. From 1:00 to 3:00 I ate lunch and took a nap. From 3:00 to 7:00 my mother tutored me. Then from 7:00 to 8:45 at night I studied the Bible with Christian, the son of Daddy's best friend Steven. Then it was off to bed to do it all again. I loved it all; not just my teaching and the training, but spending this time with my mother, father, Steven and Christian.

The other best thing about how I grew up was that my weekends were my personal time. Saturdays I could do almost anything I wanted. I was allowed to be a child and have fun like the normal child. The only rule for Saturdays is that I wasn't allowed to train. But I was too restless not to be doing something physical. So I picked up basketball and began secretly looking for places to shoot hoops and play some one-on-one. All the while, my sisters were playing with their baby dolls and beginning to have little male friends around.

For a while, I was content with my weekly training. But then I started to think I was missing something. I was getting curious about school. Much as I liked my lessons with Mom, I was ready to experience the learning environment I kept hearing my sisters talking about. So I asked my father when I could go to school.

"Well, Karma, I'd planned for your training to be only home school. You have so much lethal training in you that if you were to get into a fight with another child, you could hurt them very badly. Even kill them. We can't have that, Karma."

This made me sad. "Daddy," I said, looking up at him, "I wouldn't do anything to hurt anybody, I promise. Unless my life is in danger, I won't fight anybody at my school. I promise."

He thought about this for a minute. I was afraid I might have made him mad. "OK, Karma," he said at last. "You can go to school. But if any kid gets hurt by you, in any way, then you will be back to home school. Understand?"

I wanted to smile, but something told me I should look just as serious as he did. "Yes, Father."

"Now go play!"

I was so excited about school I rushed to find my sisters. I wanted to ask them about everything I needed to know about school. I wanted to understand all the excitement that comes with going to school. Kayren told me the girly things; Sariah and Kariah told me the ways you can get in trouble at school. Tennessee just said I would be fine, because I'd have my sisters to protect me. Then, of course, Santana had something smart to say. "Karma, your little ass isn't going to last a week in school! With your bad attitude and sneaky ways, Father is going to put you back in home school forever."

That made me so mad I forgot the rules about how to talk. "Fuck you, Santana." I stomped off to my room.

Kayren rushed after me and tried to offer some comfort. "Karma, we all are different in some ways. But we've got to accept ourselves for who we are, because only you can live and die with yourself. Understand me, little sister?"

"Yes, I do!" Kayren was so mature and humble; she reminded me of my father. She was only sixteen but gave the advice of a forty-year-old woman. I always connected with Kayren, and that day I decided that I would always be there for her, just as she was for me. "If anybody ever hurts you," I told her, "I will hurt them just as much! As for Santana, I'm thinking about paying someone to slap the shit out of her ass if she keeps messing with me."

Kayren brushed off my words. "Such harsh talk for a six-year-old. You have so much love and hate for Santana."

She had one thing right: I did both love and hate Santana. But when she ignored what I said about protecting her, I knew then she was completely clueless. Little did she know that her little sister was being trained to kill. None of my sisters knew the truth about me or about our father, that he was one of the top killers in the world.

We kept our identity discreet enough to fool even our own family. We lived everyday life just like the average person would. Just with lots of cash. Life was great for my father. He was always ready to brag to Steven about me and how fast I learned. Just a week away from his confession time, he was already writing a list of accomplishments and questions for Steven. Even though Christian and I met five days a week, my father and Steven met on business only once a month. Of course, they did hang out some, and were always attending each other's family functions. But unless it was an extreme emergency, they would never talk about business at those times. So even if my father was anxious to confess his sins and to confirm my strengths and weaknesses, he had to wait.

So in the meanwhile, he signed me up for school, a week ahead of the first day of class. I was so excited and grateful for my father's decision that I trained extra hard. studied more and slept less. I wanted to be smart as the other kids my age. I worried that they would be ahead of me. I'd never been to preschool; and my teacher was just my mom. Yeah, she was a college professor, but what did I know? I was six. What's college to a six-year-old?

Chapter 2

So Sincere with Eva

My mother and father didn't meet like the average couple. "Simple" and "exotic" were right up their alley. Before they met, they already had things in common; one of those was being a mixed race. My father was Dominican and black. My mother was Latino and white.

Plus they both loved basketball, which takes us to where they met. It was at an Orlando Magic game. On the way in, my father noticed a beautiful woman and had to ask her name.

"Eva," she answered.

"Hello, Eva my name is Sincere. I just had to let you know how beautiful you are." And with that, he walked away.

Eva went her way as well, after accepting the compliment. She was still smiling about this charming stranger as she sat down to watch the game. It was a good one. First quarter, the Magic down by two; second quarter up by four, third quarter down by six. The home crowd went wild when Orlando won 68 to 66. Like everybody else, my mother was cheering and celebrating the win until she noticed that one particular player was looking nervous, not sharing in his teammates' happiness. Then she realized the player had a bright red dot in the middle of his forehead. She tried to scream, to warn him, but before she could get a breath out, the player was falling back from a gunshot right above his eyes. Everyone in the crowd started screaming and running for the exits, sweeping Eva along with them.

She was almost to the main entrance when a man suddenly turned around and bumped into her. It was the man who had complemented her before the game. She didn't connect this right away with the swarm of police who were coming in the door. This handsome stranger pulled her toward him and kissed her. The touch of his lips made Eva forget for a second that she'd just seen a man shot. Now maybe the way I heard the story, long afterward, some details were left out. Like how they introduced themselves to each other after that first kiss. But what I did hear was that, as soon as they had kissed, they left the arena in each other's arms. The police didn't pay them any attention as they went to my father's car.

"You are fast for this to only be our first date, Mr. Sincere."

"This is not even our first date," he answered.

Eva smiled. "Well, I'd hate to see you on your third week in the game."

Amazed that so much personality came with such beauty, he began to laugh at her joke as she invited him to go out for a drink. "I haven't laughed like that in years," he told her. Something else he told her that night was his full name. Sincere Commander. Strange as that sounded to Eva, she knew it wasn't a joke.

They must have hit it off, major league. Because three months later, Eva was pregnant with their first child. They named her Kayren. With a new baby in the mix, Sincere had to stay on his grind. He began to work extra hours but still gave Eva the love and attention she needed.

I know now that she sometimes questioned his career. But Sincere would charm her and change the subject. Three years and three kids later they were happily living in Miami. Everything was going great—other than the little problem of how each of them earned a living. Sincere wanted Eva to be a stay-home mom.

Still, Eva was determined to not let her master's degree go to waste. She ended up teaching sociology at the University of Miami. Sincere was proud, sure. But he also was feeling some type of way about that. He allowed Eva to do her job, and he continued to do his job, which was another reason they had disagreements. Basically, Sincere wouldn't tell her how he made a living. Eva was nowhere near stupid; she saw they were living too large for his job to be legal. Even lawyers didn't live like they did.

While she was bringing home an OK salary from the university, Sincere brought a six million dollar house. It included ten bedrooms, six bathrooms, a ten-car garage, two guest houses, an inside/outside pool and plenty of yard space. He filled up that garage with two Mercedes (his and hers), two Range Rovers (his and hers), two motorcycles and a family van. Eva began to question Sincere more and more and, like always, Sincere would avoid giving an answer about his secret career. For a month, the arguments got worse. Eva felt like she deserved to know important things about his life; his career was one of them.

Here's how she was thinking about it. She has three of his kids and maybe someday she would become his wife. What's so bad about his job that he can't tell her? Eva wanted to know just what is going on. So one particular day she put the kids in the guest house, made sure they were asleep and went to the main house to go to Sincere's ass. (Now don't get it twisted. Yes, my mother was very educated, and in the streets she was a lady. But you piss that lady off? She's coming for you. Straight boxing style. Which was one of her hobbies, back in her day.)

Sincere greeted Eva at the door. "Hey, baby! How was work? Where the kids? And why do you have on boxing gloves?"

With no words, Eva cocked her fist back and punched Sincere square in the face.

"What the . . . Eva! What are you doing?"

"I'm tired of your shit, Sincere! Tell me the truth! Where you work?" Eva cocked back and delivered another hit to his face.

"Stop, Eva!" His nose was bleeding now.

"No, Sincere, tell me the truth." She held her stance, gloves up, ready to give him another.

Sincere didn't speak right away. Through his own pain, he began to see the hurt in her face. He could really lose her because of a secret he had to keep.

Eva shook her head slowly. Not letting her guard down, she turned to walk away.

Sincere yelled, "I'm a professional agent. For basketball players. I do illegal things for them."

Eva stopped and turned back toward him, eyebrows raised.

"Like if they want to dog fight," he went on. "I set up the bets and make sure it can't be traced to the player."

"Oh, really Sincere? Are you freaking kidding me? You know damn well I wouldn't have cared about that." She let her fists drop.

"Baby, I thought you might think it would have ruined your career," he said. "And it's possible this job could get me jail time."

Eva crossed her arms over her chest. "Sincere, you should have told me that before. I'm going to sleep with the kids in the guest house. The camera shows Kayren's about to wake up. Good night, Sincere!"

As Eva left the main crib, Sincere began to follow.

"No. You sleep alone tonight. I want you to know how it feels to be alone for a night. Because if you continue to keep secrets, this is how you will be. Once again. Good night, Sincere."

He knew she was pissed. She just needed some time to cool off, he told himself. No problem; he could allow her to have her night to herself with the kids. By the next morning, though, Sincere felt like he'd lost part of his heart. He rushed over to the guest house to find Eva and the kids were gone. The only thing he found was a note.

I don't believe your lying ass. And until you tell the truth, your kids and I will be staying somewhere else.

PS. Even if you tell the truth and I come back to your lying ass, YOU STILL WON'T GET ANY SEX FROM ME FOR A WHILE! Now go become your lie and try to dogfight that.

Panicky, Sincere began to search. Three hours later, he found Eva and the three kids. He calmly knocked on the Saver 8 room's door. When Eva opened it, she couldn't hide her amazement at seeing Sincere standing there.

"How did you find me? I thought it would be harder for you, since I was in this cheap hotel. I figured you'd look in the high-priced rooms."

When Sincere replied, she could see the anger in his eyes. "Don't you ever take my kids away from me again. Ever, Eva! Do you understand me?" Tears began to fall from his eyes.

Eva knew then she had truly struck a nerve. "Sincere, I don't want to threaten you with your own kids. But if you don't tell me what you do for us to have the luxury we have, I will leave you and take the kids with me."

Sincere knew she was telling the truth. Eva had a great job and a clean record. And Sincere damn sure didn't want to have to be telling a judge about what he did for a living. He knew that could come up in court if he and Eva ended up fighting over the kids. He didn't want to lose her. And he still wanted one of his kids to follow in his footsteps. He thought through the pros and cons and decided to confess.

"Eva," he said, "come here. I need to tell you something, but the kids don't need to hear it." Eva stepped out of the motel room and quietly shut the door behind her. Sincere led her into a stairwell where they could talk without anyone noticing.

He took her by the shoulders and looked her in the eyes. "I never wanted to lay this on you, but now I see I got to. You ready for this?"

She stared right back at him and nodded.

"OK." Sincere took a deep breath and let it out. "I'm a contract killer."

He saw her eyes go wide, but she didn't flinch. She held his gaze. "Go on."

"At first I was killing for missions only, but then I got caught up in the game."

"What do you mean, 'caught up'?"

"I kill people who've done horrible, terrible crimes to hurt other people. Like child molesters and any type of sick-minded people like that. I kill people who done wrong even if there's no money involved. I call it 'on-Earth human karma.' But it's not just a duty; it's something I have to do. It's an addiction."

As Eva took this in, the look on Sincere's face seemed like relief, as if to say, 'OK, now you know!' At first Eva couldn't speak. She was lost in thought. Then, blinking away tears, she pulled him closer and embraced him. She whispered in his left ear, "All I got to say is two things. I need a favor; and prepare for twins."

~

After they got home from the Saver 8, everything felt different. Both knew they still had plenty to talk about.

Sincere sat down, looked at Eva and said, "Now, let's talk about this favor."

That's when she began to confide in him about her early life, going back to the days she was a teenager. Her mother, Eva told Sincere, was once a beautiful and intelligent woman. Then she met Julian. He was a big-time drug dealer, who had influenced her mother to use heavy drugs and drink heavily, too. All of that had played a part in her downfall, Eva explained. "But the major reason this piece of human trash deserves to die is because he would beat my mother. For years. Get her high and drunk, then rape her and even piss on her."

Sincere listened silently, thinking through exactly how he would grant this favor.

"One night, Julian got drunk," Eva went on, "and beat her so bad that she got brain damage. She's been fighting for two years now, but I just got word she has only six months to live.

"I want him dead. Can you do this mission for me? Please?"

Sincere answered softly, "Never say 'please' when it comes to ever needing anything from me. He's a dead man walking from now on!

"Now I need one thing from you." Sincere got down on one knee and pulled out a little velvet case. He opened it to show her a dazzling engagement ring. "Will you marry me?"

Chapter 3

"Till Death do us part"

After a short hesitation, Eva said yes. They were married a month later, on June 24, 1998. It was a small wedding in their back yard, by the beach. The only guests were Sincere's brother from California and his best friend Steven, who was a well-known pastor in Florida. Eva had her mother there. Sincere paid big money to set things up so her mother could attend. That alone made the moment perfect for Eva.

"Sincere," Pastor Steven asked, "Do you take Eva to be your wife, till death do you part? Eva, do you take Sincere Commander to be your husband, till death do you part?" With those words, Eva and Sincere were officially married.

Now it was time to get down to business. While Sincere was ready for his kill, Eva insisted that he be patient. He obeyed her wishes and began getting ready for their honeymoon. Eva picked Jamaica; this excited Sincere, who had never been there. He was already imaging the two weeks alone with his new wife. Eva set up the whole honeymoon plan. Their first day in Jamaica consisted of back massages, swimming with dolphins, and a private candle light dinner on a boat anchored just off the beach. After dinner, they made love on the deck while watching the stars.

The next morning, they sat down to breakfast in a five-star restaurant Eva had picked out. She asked for a table near the window, with a view out onto a sunny outdoor dining area. Once they placed their orders, she carefully began to talk about her stepfather. "Baby, remember when I was telling you how my stepfather was a big-time dope dealer?"

This got Sincere's attention. "Yes, baby, I remember. Why?"

"Well, you see, he's not like the average dealer. He is a huge-time dope dealer. Julian has hundreds of connections. Security, too. It's definitely going to be hard to get close to him, let alone kill him."

Sincere looked at Eva with surprise. How could she question his abilities as a contract killer? Confidently, Sincere said, "Eva, baby, I've been killing since I was twelve. I'm far from stupid; I have my masters in criminal justice and my minor in massage therapy. Yeah, babes; that's why your back's never sore."

Eva's look was a challenge: Prove it.

"Eva, I could kill that man over there." He nodded through the glass toward a man at a corner table out on the patio, surrounded by a crew of beefy guys in shades. "The one who's sitting with all that security. I'm one of the top five best contract killers in the world. Not just the country or the state. The whole world."

Eva's smile was loving but sarcastic. "Great, baby, because that's who you're here to kill. That's Julian."

Sincere took another quick look at the man, then looked back at Eva, her face dead serious. He touched her hand and smiled. "Check, please." Back at their condo, Sincere heard more about the mysterious honeymoon plans Eva had made. "Wow. I couldn't have set this up any better. I love you baby! Tell me more."

"Well," Eva explained, "he moved here to Jamaica when he found out he had a warrant for his arrest; been here ever since."

Sincere realized Eva had done her homework. Now it was time for him to do his. For four days, Sincere followed Julian's every move. By the fourth day, Sincere knew when and where Julian ate, who his contacts were, where his deals went down, and, last but not least, when was the best time to kill him. Like Eva said, Julian was well known. Even in his own organization, there were people who wanted him dead. Julian was a murderer and a rapist. He had shit on plenty of the people on his payroll. So all Sincere had to do was pay off the right members of Julian's crew and his mission was set up, easy. Money talks, bullshit walks, Sincere would often say.

Eva was excited and nervous about their joint mission. Three days later the mission was successfully completed. Eva felt relieved that her stepfather's life finally ended and that chapter in her life was closed. She also felt relief to know her family could be protected forever.

Sincere was proud that he'd been able to do this for the woman he was deeply in love with. He knew then this was the woman he was going to spend his life with. Till death do them part.

Chapter 4

The birth of Karma

After the twins were born Eva wanted to get her tubes tied. Think about it: seven years already, five kids; it was time to slow down for a little. So one Sunday night after dinner Eva brought the matter to Sincere's attention.

Without a second of thought he refused, but went on with questions and reasons for why they shouldn't stop having children. "Eva, we have enough money to support a family of twenty, with extra money to spend! Our marriage is happy. Our kids are happy!"

That gave Eva an opening to plead her case. "But part of me is not happy," she told him. "I work, I take care of the kids and I am a great mother. I just want to experience some life without being pregnant!"

Sincere took a deep breath. "Baby, I understand. We will slow down. But not quit."

From that conversation alone, Eva was content, convinced she wouldn't have another child for at least four to five more years. But just two years later, she was pregnant once again.

Sincere was excited. He had always wanted a huge family and this was about to add another member to it.

Eva wasn't so happy. During her pregnancy she had major complications. She was sick most of the time with high fever and severe headaches. Even though Sincere took care of her through her hard times, it wasn't enough. On top of all the pregnancy complications, the baby turned out to be autistic. They named her Destiny

Eva and Sincere knew that they were going to have difficulties taking care of Destiny. Still, they wanted to do it alone without any outside help. They wanted Destiny to have a normal life, just like the other kids. My father didn't treat her any different. He pulled major strings to put her in special programs and a special class that both he and my mother felt were the best for her.

After all the complications with the last birth, Eva and Sincere decided to slow down again. Eva decided she would have no more kids at all and began taking birth control on the down-low.

Sincere continued to kill for a living and make millions. He knew he was going to have to retire soon and it was about time for him to have another child to continue the tradition. Kayren was five now and about to head to school. After that, he knew, time would move so fast. And that meant he had to come up with a plan, quick. First, Sincere figured, he would continue to work. He would also work on making another baby. So now he needed to convince Eva to have one more child, which somehow he knew for sure would be a baby boy.

At first, Eva was like, "Hell, no!"

But, of course, Sincere with his charm convinced her again. A year and three months after Destiny was born, Eva was once again pregnant. Fully expecting his seventh child to be a boy, Sincere was extra excited. He brought all kinds of gadgets for a baby boy. He even worked out a year-by-year plan for training his new-born, all the way up to the age of twenty-one. This time, all of Eva's doctor visits went well. Both were ready for the August 13 due date. Sincere felt like that was now his lucky number. Everything was going great until they found out a hurricane was on the way. Sincere did what he could to prepare for the storm and prayed that the baby would wait, not coming until after the storm had passed. Well, that night his prayers were not answered. At a minute past midnight on August 13, 1998, I was ready to come out.

You think I cared about a damn hurricane? No way! I was ready. And thirty minutes later, Sincere was rushing Eva to the hospital for me to be born. Sincere didn't want to drive because of all the weather chaos, but he had no choice. I was on my way. I damn sure wasn't waiting on any ambulance. So through all the heavy rain, broken branches, eighty miles an hour wind—and let's not forget the power failures—Sincere was still able to get Eva safely to the hospital for the doctors to help deliver me. The storm had the doctors and nurses working at a fast pace, treating people with gunshot wounds, overdoses and injuries from car accidents and the hurricane. Still, no one there was preparing for a baby except Sincere and Eva. All around them, nurses and doctors were running all over the place.

All Sincere saw was happiness. All he heard was silence. In his mind nothing else mattered but his wife and his baby to be. Sincere felt peace of mind while the doctors took Eva to the delivery room.

A few moments later the doctor stuck his head into the waiting room and said, "Let's go deliver your baby boy."

When Sincere got to the room he found Eva laid out to deliver. "Sincere, I fucking hate you."

The doctor reassured him, "That's normal for her to say that."

Sincere replied, "This is her seventh time giving birth and she never said that."

The nurse laughed. Sincere recognized her outspoken attitude. "Well, then, she fucking hates you."

Amazed, Sincere stared at the nurse, then turned to his wife and said, "I fucking love you."

Eva turned away; that sincere act wasn't working tonight. Twenty minutes later they were in the last moments. Eva was screaming and nurses and doctors were hustling back and forth. The lights were flickering off and on because the generators were losing power. Sincere saw fear in Eva's eyes as she turned to him and whispered, "I love you."

Then loud beeping from a monitor told him that her heart stopped. In a panic, Sincere turned to the doctor and yelled, "Somebody help my wife!" The lights turned off and for sixty seconds all he heard was silence. Then a dim emergency light came on, and a nurse's voice said, "One, two, three, clear! One, two, three, clear!"

"Don't give up on me," Sincere called out.

"One, two, three, clear!" Eva's upper body lifted up like she was gasping for air and the doctor said, "Push, Eva." Sincere heard Eva pushing and soon, in the dim light, he saw two very important things: his wife breathing and his new baby girl.

In the doctor's arms, in silence, I looked calm and at peace. Sincere was so happy that he didn't realize he was once again a father to a baby girl. Then, ten minutes later, he came to his senses and began to feel a little disappointed.

In spite of his fake smiles and extra excitement, Eva saw right through his emotions. "You know," she said, "you can still train her to become your mini-you."

Sincere replied, "But Eva, she needs to be protected like her sisters. She needs to become a doctor or a lawyer. Not a professional killer."

"Wasn't your mother one?"

Feeling frustrated, but struggling to stay calm, Sincere replied, "That's different, Eva."

Eva sighed and reached for Sincere's hand. "You will know if she's the one."

That whole stormy night my father stared at me. All types of thought and questions were going through his mind. He was so confused and only had a little time. If he had planned for the training to start on time then he had to decide in two days, which was my mother's release date. Sincere was confused about a lot of things, but he was certain that he wanted to hold me. Lying in the dark, Sincere put me in his arms while lying in the dark. I was still silent from birth. All I did was follow his head movements with my eyes. Sincere was amazed that I didn't take my eye off him. I barely blinked.

Then a loud knock hit the door and that damn outspoken-ass nurse came in. "Hey, congratulations! I know I laughed at you and all earlier, but the doc told me that if I don't apologize then I might get wrote up again, and it's the fifth time this month, and I need this job. So, I'm sorry." Sincere didn't know if that was an apology or a confession but either way he accepted it. After the nurse left, my father turned back to me and was astonished to see me still looking at him. Not once did I take my eyes off him. He knew then that I was the one.

"Eva, we will name her Karma."

Chapter 5

Karma's nursery

Two days later, my mother was getting me ready to leave the hospital and my father was preparing for my arrival. He was extra excited to get started and my sisters were even more excited to see me. I, on the other hand, might not have been going anywhere because I still hadn't cried yet. The doctors and nurses were amazed, and still more curious about why. So they gave me a lot of tests. Still, no crying. They told my mom that I was a normal, healthy baby who will cry when it's time.

"Will she ever cry?"

"We don't know."

After we were released, my father was already prepared to take me to the quiet room. That was my training house in the back yard, which he'd had built especially for me. But for right now, it was my quiet room. Only used for silence. The plan was for two weeks only my mother and me would be in the quiet room. Neither my father nor my sisters were allowed to enter. My father's plan was to fill my mind with peace while I bonded with my mother. The second two weeks, my family could come see me, but without speaking. That was the first step in my training. My second step wouldn't start till I was one. So for the first month I was in the quiet room.

The other eleven months of my first year I spent with my family, just like an average child. Every weekend, I had to go into the quiet room, but now it was with my father instead of my mother. At first, he didn't do any major training. All he would do was sit quietly and hold me in his arms, admiring how I focused on him. It was like I already knew it was my destiny to obey my father's orders.

On my first birthday, I got baptized by Steven at his church then Mom and Daddy prepared a celebration. All eleven members of our family were there. They weren't blood kin, but Steven and his son Christian were as much a part of the family as my father's nine. Steven had plenty of reasons for being at the celebration. His main reason was to introduce me to Christian, who had been born the same month as I was.

For a few hours, I played and enjoyed my party. Then my father announced, "OK Karma, time to get to work!"

His first rule of training was no diapers. So nine months after my first birthday I was trained to use the bathroom. My mother was in charge of this. In the meantime, my father was preparing my weapons. He already had knives and guns ready for when I got to my teenage years. But first, I needed some for my childhood. He figured I could start off with plastic, then work my way up to razor blades and aluminum bats.

After getting my toys straight, my father went to the church to confess his sins to his pastor, who was Steven. "Forgive me, Father, for I have sinned."

"Again, Sincere?"

Sincere replied, "Hello. Steven?"

"Hello, Sincere. I was just thinking about you. I have a mission that is in need of your assistance. But first, confess your sins."

"Father, Karma is ready. I think with our guidance she can really become the best assassin ever in the world. But I'm still uncertain about my ultimate three rules for her to follow."

"Why don't you give her the same rules you had?" Steven asked.

"Well, my rules, as you know, are heartless. Already, she doesn't cry. So I have to come up with something so she'll have a heart."

"You will make the right decision," Steven assured him.

"Is Christian preparing as well?"

"You know it! As soon as he can read, he'll be learning the Bible, just as I've planned."

"Great!" Sincere said. "So let's get to this mission we have in hand."

Steven explained, "Well, there's a young man name Alexander who's selling a lot of hard drugs in the neighborhood. Just because of his drug game, the rates of crime and killings have gone up thirty percent. More kids are being born as crack and heroin babies. He must be stopped." After a minute to be sure his words had sunk in, Steven went on. "Sincere, you know that this is always the last resort. I went through protocol. I asked him to stop the drug selling. And of course he refused. He used violence towards me and threw me out of his place of business. And so he leaves us no other choice. He has to go!"

"How soon?"

"ASAP." Steven added, "You also have a half-million-dollar reward for your success."

"Say no more."

After his "confession," my father was feeling great. He always felt great after a confession with his best friend, who was one of the top preachers in Florida. Sincere had known Steven since they were just a year old. Both were also raised up in the family business. They met through Sincere's father, who was also a contract killer, and Steven's dad, who was a preacher, too. As they grew up, both boys were trained to connect with each other but still live different lives. How each generation shaped the next was a chain reaction that I didn't understand until it was too late. But that's something to tell in a later chapter of this story. Anyway, as you can see, Sincere and Steven grew up with a bond that would last forever.

For my first four years, my training was simple. I ran, but two miles a day. I swam two laps a day. And I played with the little weapons I'd earned through the years. Mentally, I was praying every night and getting schooled by my mother. My three rules were to Protect, Obey, and Love. Each of these had special guidance and meaning for all of us.

I must protect. Who? My mother, my father, my sisters and any others who have a good heart!

I must obey God, Mother, Father. And Christian. At first I didn't know why I had to obey Christian, but my father said, "In time, you will find out."

Last, but not least in my opinion, the most important rule was love. I must love everyone to a certain level. I had to learn how to figure people out, to read their minds to figure out what level of love they're on. I learned about three love levels. First and greatest was what my parents called the Ultimate love, which automatically included God, my mother, my father, and Christian. Others could be added, but with my approval only. The second was affectionate love, which my father didn't explain too much at the time. That's funny to me now. Maybe because I was only four, and even though I was about to become the best killer in the world, I was still his little girl.

To my father, this was the most important part of the Love rules: Life or Death Love. In what I do, it's so important to understand how to compare and contrast the two. I could only harm someone if my mother or father, my sisters or any civilians were in harm's way. Father didn't want to teach me how to kill yet. That would come in due time.

So in the meantime, I was just training and living an average life like the other kids. I would fight with them and play practical jokes on them from time to time. My father wanted to make sure that I lived as a normal kid. I didn't have a problem with acting normal; I just had a problem with liking the things a normal child would like. For example, average kids like toys, video games, and simple stuff like that. I, on the other hand, liked guns, knives, and any type of sharp objects. But I adjusted to the normal child's life as much as possible. My sisters and I fought like average kids—Except that they would all try to gang up on me so they could set me up. I would play jokes, too, and set them up for all kinds of pranks. It was all in fun, of course. Until Mom found Santana tied up in a closet. She had been there an hour. After that, Mom forced my father to keep me busy. He didn't mind that.

I was five now, with a mean mouth. Plus attitude. Daddy wanted to correct that, but he had to stay focused. His focus now was that it was time to start me using lethal weapons. Even though he had me on combat training mode, he still was conscientious about my wellbeing. He would test me to my limit, but that was never as far as I knew he could go.

So on my sixth birthday, I decided to prove my strength. The best place to do, I thought, would be at the water park in Atlanta that was my birthday present from Mom and Daddy. Of course, my six sisters were excited and ready for this trip. It had been forever since my parents had been there. It was also our first time going as a family. As soon as we got there I was ready to show Daddy my talents. What I had planned out was to pick the park's biggest slide, jump off the edge and into the water without anyone noticing. For a little humor, I figured I'd pull Santana to the bottom without her realizing it was me until "Mission Accomplished." I always picked Santana to mess with because, ever since I was born, she was the one who always messed with me. So my mission was planned. Now it was time to complete. At first we went to the kiddy pool so Destiny could have fun. While she was playing, I tugged at Daddy's shirt and asked, "Can you take me to the big slide?"

Of course, Santana, being nosy, was listening to the conversation and had to comment. "Karma, you too scared to go on a big slide. I don't have time to get embarrassed by my little sister."

And, of course, I replied, "Whatever, Santana! I bet you won't go!"

As Santana and I were mean mugging, eye to eye, Daddy yelled, "Let's go. if you're ready for the big slide."

Mom whispered to him, "Are you sure they're ready for such a big slide?"

Daddy looked at her, smiled and turned away. "Let's go, girls."

On the way, I was so excited, I couldn't stop smiling. Santana, on the other hand, was looking a little nervous. I could feel her fear, and I wanted her to feel more before we got there. So I whispered, "I heard when you're going down that big slide, the water sucks you down to the bottom." I gave her a moment to think about that. "Some come back up . . . and some don't." Oh, that did it.

Santana slapped me in the head and as usual we started fighting but this only lasted for seconds. Daddy was right there to break us up and straighten us out. After the long walk, it was time to complete the mission. Santana being Santana, she wanted to go first, which was my plan from the start. As soon as she got the "Go" she began to slide. Without hesitation, I jumped off the edge of slide. Only the operator and my father saw the jump, and neither could stop me. I was already in action. I dropped twelve feet to where the slide crossed under itself the first time. The jump went perfectly and I landed exactly where I had planned—ahead and downstream from my sister. Santana was five seconds behind. Before she knew it, she was hitting the water. What she didn't expect was to feel a little hand grab her leg and pull her to the bottom. Santana tried to scream but the water filled her mouth. All you could see at first was her hands leaving the water surface. Then, ten seconds later, she was floating back up, coughing and gagging, with tears coming from her eyes. I swam up from the bottom and came up on the other side of the pool, smiling. The operator wasn't happy at all. He ran from the top of the slide, yelling in a panic. He really thought I was dead, which was on my mind for a second before I did it I just didn't care. I was determined to prove to my father that I was ready for extreme training, not any more small stuff.

He got the point. He was very proud of the mission I had accomplished, but he wasn't happy that I'd scared the pure shit out of Savanna. I really didn't care about her feelings at the time, but I always believed that I should obey and follow my father's words. Those words were ready to be spoken when we got home from the water park. "Karma, you can't put fear in your sisters and/or hurt them in any way. I, your mother and your sisters are all the family you got. You must have a bond with your sisters! I know there will be times when you'll disagree and even fight; but remember: they always should win. You are ten times stronger than them, so please keep that in mind. You could have drowned your sister today. You must remember to be willing to kill for them if necessary but not ever kill them; not physically, mentally or emotionally. Understand?"

This confused me. I asked, "What is 'kill," Daddy?"

"Well, we weren't going to talk about it until your tenth birthday but after what happened today, I feel you're more advanced than I ever imagined. So it's time to teach. For the rest of your life, you're going to know the ways to kill a human being. And while you're learning this, you will also learn the Bible." In his office, Sincere took down a tall frame that held one of my baby pictures. Behind the picture was a safe with a digital lock. He punched in an eight-digit code and pulled out the most beautiful Bible I have ever seen. We go to Uncle Steven's church every Sunday and I have seen lots of Bibles but nothing as fine as this one. "Karma, I want you to guide your life with this Bible. One of your permanent goals is to have read the whole Bible and understand it as much as possible before you reach the age of twenty five. If you have any questions about the Bible, you can feel free to ask Christian. If he doesn't know, when Steven isn't busy, ask him. Understand?"

"Yes, Daddy. But I have one question. What is 'kill'?"

My father's expression turned serious. "Before I tell you what it is, you must promise me that you will not tell anyone! Especially not Steven and Christian. Not until the time is right. Promise?"

"I promise, Daddy!"

"Well, then: let the training began!"

Chapter 6

Living and learning

It was finally time for school and I was extra excited. I got all jigged up and was ready to make moves.

"Hold up, little sister," Kayren yelled as I went to walk out the door. "We got to eat breakfast!"

I was so excited I'd forgotten to eat. The thought of being able to be a kid and have my cover mode on for a longer time had me so excited. Now, don't get me wrong. I loved my training and the serious methods I was learning, but still, from time to time, I wanted to be a kid and have some fun. Kick a kid's ass or two. Ha! I'm just playing. But I did plan to play a few games while I was in school. Just the thought alone had me too ready for school to eat, but still I tried. While I was eating a pancake and a couple of sausage links, I could tell my father was a little nervous but still proud of me. On my way out the door, I gave Mom a huge hug and my father, as well. Even though he had major confidence in me, he still had to remind me how well trained I was and that I should never use any of my skills until he told me it was time. After his small speech, he kissed me on the forehead and sent me on my way. I jumped into the car with Kayren, the twins and destiny.

My elementary school was down the street from Kayren's high school. Santana's and Tennessee's middle school was walking distance from our house. Here we go, off to school! As soon as I saw the school, my first thought was, "Wow! My house is about the same size."

"Ok guys, be good!"

I looked back, gave Kayren a wink and said, "Don't worry, big sis, I got this all under control!" I walked Destiny to her classroom, where all the special kids went. Right away, I knew by the way the other kids were picking at my sis that I was going to have to run this school so she would be protected. I already knew I couldn't do it all in one day but in a few weeks it would be taken care of. I kissed Destiny on the cheek and told her not to worry about the punk ass kids; "Little sister got it all under control."

As soon as I got the words out my mouth, here comes some little bitch who shouts out, "AWWWWWW, look at the dykes! LMAO!"

Shocked, I looked over my shoulder and answered, "You just mad cause your daddy left your mom for a man!"

That made her mad. She began to come towards me and Destiny, yelling, "Bitch, my daddy left my mom for a woman, not a man!"

I pulled Destiny behind me, yelling back, "That's what your momma told you, but your daddy really laid up with your so-called uncle Ron Ron. I'm sure Ron Ron look better than your mother. If I had to lay beside your mother for all those years, I would have left too."

That bitch was too stuck after I said that. All she could do was swing and punch me right in the face, as hard as she could. I began to laugh. Before I could retaliate, the principal got in the middle and broke it up.

"Kids! Stop all this nonsense! Passion, you're supposed to be in the fifth grade hallway anyway! I better not see you back here again. Understand?"

Passion looked at the principal with a slick face and said, "Yes, ma'am." But while walking past me, she gave a hard bump and whispered, "It's not over."

All I could do was give her a sarcastic wink and shake my head. Little did she know I wasn't planning for this to be over, either. I was just getting started. With a smile, the principal bent down, looked me in the face and said, "Are you OK? You must be new. Passion loves to pick on the younger kids."

"Younger kids, huh?"

That made her smile even more. "Looks like you're not scared a bit. What's your name and your teacher's name, little miss?"

"Karma. My name is Karma! And my teacher's name is Mrs. Campbell. Like the soup."

"Mrs. Campbell? Well! Her class is right down this hall, to the left. You're going to enjoy her. She is a really nice lady!"

"OK. Thanks."

"Take care, Karma, and be safe out here at Sunshine Elementary School of Excellence." She straightened up, then looked down at me again to make sure I got the message.

I looked up at her with a message of my own. "Do me a favor," I said. "Tell these other kids to be careful, too."

She seemed a little shocked at this, but didn't say anything.

I tried my best not to converse with her too long and not to look like no snitch, so I had to keep it moving and find my class. I was already late.

As soon as I entered the room all the kids turned and stared. "Hello, Karma!" the teacher said. "I've been expecting you. Class, say hello to Karma."

"HELLO KARMA," the class yelled, along with little giggles and smirks.

I looked around. With a straight face, I said, "What's up?" I had to get my mean mug on; didn't want these kids thinking I'm a punk. So I kept it short and simple while walking to my assigned seat.

Class went well. When it was time to pick up Destiny, I already prepared myself for the fifth-grade bully who called herself Passion. I walked down the hall to pick up Destiny and, to my surprise, there was no Passion. When we got outside I still saw no Passion. I was a little disappointed, because I wanted to whip that ass, but then on the other hand, I didn't want to get in any trouble. I had promised my father to be good unless someone messed with me. Now don't get me wrong; I didn't want to hurt her badly, at least not to the point of hospital care, but I did want to whip that ass kindergarten style.

While we waited for Kayren to come pick us up, I got a text from my father saying to go to the high school and wait for Kayren to get out of volleyball practice. So Destiny and I began to walk. Thirty-eight seconds later, I began to notice someone was following, so I told Destiny to keep walking while I played hide and seek with the stalker behind us. Destiny was always a big listener; she did what her little sister told her to. I climbed a tree so whoever was following couldn't see me. As soon as she walked by, I jumped from the tree and landed straight on her back with my blade. Destiny turned around, still thinking it's a game, clapping and yelling, "You got her, sister! Yayyy! We won!" I looked up and blinked my eye to reassure Destiny that we were in no harm, then looked back down at Passion. "You trying to kill me and my sister? Bitch, I'm crazy! I will fuck you and your family up! You hear me?"

In tears, Passion replied, "I'm sorry! I'm soooooooooo sorry!"

I began to mash her head in the sand while yelling, "Bitch, you not sorry! If you was sorry, you would have stopped this morning. But noooooooooo, you want to follow me and my sister. Destiny, I think we should kill her!"

Passion screamed, "Please don't kill me! I promise I will do anything you want!"

That made me smile. "Anything?"

"Yes! Anything! Please don't kill me!!"

"Bitch, we not talking 'bout that anymore. You said you'll do anything if I let you live; I'm gonna take you up on your punk-ass offer."

"What you want me to do?"

"Simple. I know you like to pick on younger kids. Well, it's time to mess with someone your own size."

Passion looked confused. "Who?" she whimpered.

"I need you to slap a bitch for me. I'll tell you when the time is right, but for right now your life is in my hands. And don't you ever fuck with me or my sister again!"

"I won't, I promise!"

"Now look at my sister and tell her you love autistic people. You tell her they have a better and more innocent heart than any bully like you. Also tell her you okay with gay people and it's wrong to pick on people like that, And you say it like you mean it, or I'm going to kick your ass again!"

Passion repeated what I told her and I let her get up. Wiping her tears, she began to walk away. Before I went my way, I told her one last thing. "I'm six and I run this school now, chick!"

As we walked, Destiny whispered, "I'm glad we don't play hide and seek like that, Karma!" All I could do was smile. My sister was my everything but she couldn't defend herself. I knew from the start that I would have to protect her the most.

~

At first it was kind of hard adjusting to school life along with my training. Not much had changed but my school time took the place of my learning time with my mom and my training hours was moved to evenings and weekends. I still had to wake up at five a.m. to run—I was up to five miles now—and swim twenty laps before school. There were times I would get a little frustrated with school because it was so easy. I had to figure out ways to entertain myself. By the time I was three months into the school game, I was ready to set up a minor robbery mission.

I had finally found someone who I could call my best friend. Her name is Kayla. She became my hype man as well as my best friend. She had one brother and no sisters so I basically became her sister. We clicked because she was my total opposite. Her mother was out in the streets doing crack while Kayla was with her "owner," who was an alcoholic with a failing liver. He never laid a hand on her, but his drinking ways were enough abuse. Once we met in class, she clung to me and we've been great friends ever since. Even Destiny likes her!

Kayla became one of the sisters. She ate dinner with us and often stayed with us for the night. At first, my father was concerned about having her here, seeing that her parents didn't seem to care. But once he found out about her life, he accepted her like one of his own.

But even though she was a great person, Kayla was bad as hell in school. I think it was for the attention. Whatever her reasons, she couldn't ever get Mrs. Campbell's end-of-the-week treat. That was two pieces of candy if you had a good report by Friday. I always got the treat; Kayla never did. So one day I tried to talk to her, telling her to behave so she can learn better and even get her two pieces of candy. She took my advice, but the very next Friday our teacher was in a bitching mood. Because Kayla had been five minutes late for school that morning, Mrs. Campbell didn't give her the treat. I was pissed but didn't show it. Kayla, on the other hand, was crushed. She held her composure in class, but once that chick got out, it was a wrap. First one tear dropped; then they all started to fall.

For a second, I thought, "Why can't my feelings build up to the point of bringing tears?" I didn't dwell on it too much, because I was still seeing Kayla cry and it was hurting me. Finally she tired out and there was a moment of silence. That's when an idea popped into my head. "Hey, I got an idea. We just need a few soldiers."

Kayla stopped crying and looked at me. "Soldiers?"

"Yes, soldiers. I been wanting to complete a mission and I know the perfect person to rob."

"Who?"

"Our teacher, Mrs. Campbell!" Hell, yeah, I planned to rob her. She hurt my home-girl's feelings. And yes, I get candy at the end of the week, but forget that. Kayla's like my sister, so if my sister can't get candy, it's like I can't get candy.

"Karma, I'm down," she told me.

"Enough said."

All I needed now was two more. While thinking through ways to complete my mission, I ran into the terrible twins. Jamal and Jamel were two of the kids in the class who were never going to get their end-of-the-week treat. It's not like Jamal and Jamel had bad grades; they just fought too much. They really couldn't go a day without getting into an actual physical fight. Deep in my mind, I knew that might be a problem, but I didn't dwell on it too long.

So boom! We got our team. The date to attack was also set. Then Kayla began mentioning that we needed a fifth person; less chance to get caught was her reason. At first I was like, "Hell, no." We would have to split the candy five ways. But even though I didn't like the idea, I had to face the fact that she was right. So I came up with a plan to get Mrs. Campbell when she re-up her candy dish. That was the first of every month, and September 1 was just a week away. My plan was to have the twins start a fight, which happens often anyway, and have my right-hand friend Kayla looking out for the principal, ready to distract her if needed. The new girl? I only brought her in to move the chair faster while I grabbed the prizes. Once I'd done that, everything would go back to normal and Mrs. Campbell wouldn't even notice she'd been robbed until the end of the day. By then, she wouldn't know who had robbed her. And we would be in the park, splitting up the end-of-the-week treats.

A week later we were ready. That morning I woke up with a smile, confident the mission was going to be successful. For one thing, I'd been doing my homework. During my off time, I would watch the movie Set it Off and I always dreamed that I could rob someone like that. When you're young, it doesn't take much to influence and inspire you. At the time, my inspiration was this movie. This wasn't part of my training. My father never taught me how to steal; that was kind of a small trade I picked up on my own. Remember, at the age of six I was just learning about rights and wrongs.

I rushed down the stairs and greeted my father with a huge smile. "Good morning, Daddy!"

"Good morning, Karma! How was your workout this morning? You completed everything on your list, right?"

"Yes, sir. I did my five-mile run, I swam eight laps, and I also did all my pull-ups and pushups."

"Great to hear, Karma! Report card coming up soon. Hope it's just as great."

"It will be, Daddy. Promise!"

After breakfast it was time to go to school. I was so excited, it should have been obvious. Still, my father didn't pay it any attention, which was good. It was time to make our move.

Kayla and I walked Destiny to her class as usual. I got to my class just in time. "Hello, kids!" Mrs. Campbell said. "It's eight o'clock! You know what we do at eight!" Everyone stood up to sing the national anthem. After that I looked over and winked at Kayla, which meant it's time for the mission.

Kayla raised her hand. "Can I go to the bathroom?"

"Yes, Kayla, but hurry please."

Time to get started. The twins got their signal for action, too. Jamal punched Jamel and he punched back. Mrs. Campbell hurried over to break up the fight, just like I had planned. I discreetly snuck around behind where they were fighting, which put me three feet from the prize. The new girl set the chair exactly where it was supposed to be, but fifty-eight seconds later then the time she should have. I went for it anyway and jumped on the chair before I noticed the dumb new girl had gotten the teacher's rolling chair. Just as I was reaching for the prize, the chair moved, I lost my balance and I busted my ass. Candy flew all over the damn place and I fell hard on the floor. It really hurt; I lay there for at least thirty seconds. Then I realized two things. First, the teacher was too busy with the twins to notice me; and second, I had to try to get away before she did notice and I got caught. I tried to crawl but suddenly felt a strong hand grab the back of my shirt. Next thing I knew, I was hanging in the air with candy falling out of my clothes, feet dangling. Once I realized I couldn't move, this chick just hung there.

I hadn't planned on the principal, Mrs. Turner, to walk into the class. I had planned on Kayla making sure that didn't happen. After the jig was up, the twins quit fighting. Kayla came back from the bathroom way late, acting like she didn't know what was wrong. And the new girl was in a corner crying, looking all scared! The whole mission was a complete failure. I was so disappointed in my crew and scared of the soon-to-be consequences. I knew that if the principal told my father, it was possible he could take me out of school. I'd felt pretty brave before. But waiting in the principal's office for my father to come, I was really scared.

When he showed up in the office door, my father looked me straight in the eye. All I could do was put my head down and shake it. "What seems to be the problem, Mrs. Turner?"

"Well, there's really not a problem," she said. Her words surprised me almost as much as the kind way she said them. "You see, I think Karma is bored with first grade. I'm sure you realize she is way more advanced than the other children. Her grades are all A-plus. And I have never seen a child who is only six who can speak four different languages!"

"So what do you think I should do about, it Mrs. Turner?"

"Well, we have already given her a placement test. She scored at the fifth grade level. But by law, we only can skip her up two grades. So by the end of next week, we plan to place her in the third grade. To do that, however, we need your permission."

I looked up, amazed that Mrs. Turner hadn't mentioned my recent mission failure with my comrades. So before my father could get a word out I shouted, "Yes! I will move to the third grade." while thinking to myself, "I'll move to college as long as he don't tell my father how bad I've been today."

My father gave me a strong stare. "Thank you, Mrs. Turner. Please give us a day to think about it. First, I need to talk it over with her mother."

"Of course, Mr. Commander," the principal said. "I'm looking forward to hearing from you soon."

I was so excited about moving up two grades that I forgot all about the failed mission. On the way home, my father had nothing but great things to say. "Karma might be going to the third grade, huh?"

I wanted to be sarcastic, but I guess I ended up sounding like I'd conceded the point. "Maybe."

He gave me a smile. "I guess it shouldn't be a problem for you to be upgraded. But there will be no more failed missions. OK?"

At first, I smiled. Then I thought about it and looked back at him, amazed that he knew. "Daddy knows everything."

He winked and turned back to watch the road. Silently, I stared out the window, shaking my head, but I couldn't help seeing my grin reflected in the glass.

As soon as we pulled up at home, I ran up to tell my sisters the good news. "Guess what, ya'll! A chick moving to the third grade!"

A huge smile on her face, Kayren gave me a huge hug. "Congrats, little sister! I am so proud of you!"

"Thanks! The principal said there's not many that skip up a grade and I was the first to skip up two. And maybe three! What ya'll know about that!"

"Wow. They want to move this cussing, high-temper, emotionless freak up a grade?" Of course, someone had to steal my joy. Yeah, it was the one and only Santana who wanted to have that glory. "You're not smart," she said. "You just got lucky on a test."

"Yo, fuck you, Santana! You always messing with me. Someone needs to slap the hell out your ass!"

Santana took a threatening step towards me.

Tennessee stepped into her path to stop her. "Why are ya'll always fighting?"

As I began to walk away, I whispered my answer to Kayren: "Because she's an insecure bully."

Santana shouted, "And this mess about me needing to be slapped is just your imagination. It'll never happen!"

I didn't react; I just walked away. I didn't want to spoil the surprise I had for her. Plus, at the moment, I just didn't want to let her to spoil my joy.

"Karma! Time for training!" As soon as my father said that, I knew it was time to get in serious mode. On my way to the quiet room, I began to prepare myself. I knew that once I entered the training room it would be nothing but work and determination. In the quiet room, we never smiled or talked about life. It was all work. To begin, I would run. Around and around on the little indoor track in the quiet room. That was timed; I was expected to improve my time every day. Then all those pull-ups and pushups, and last but not least the swimming, in the pool between the quiet room and the main house. That was also timed. After that little warm-up, it was time for the real training with my father. I would learn how to use guns, swords, knives and everyday objects. My father taught me how to use each device in different situations, in differ-

31

ent missions. By now, at the age of six, I knew karate, ninja moves, and even street fighting. And with what I learned in the quiet room, the goal was to do everything in silence; in any situation, never get noticed!

"Karma, you shouldn't have to use any of your fighting techniques any time soon; but it's best to learn now. Your sisters are getting older and when I die it's up to you to take care of them. Maybe even kill for them." After my father's speech, I just shook it off and went to play again before it was time to study with Christian. Little did I know I was going to have to use my skills sooner than I thought.

A huge party was coming up. My oldest sister, who was sixteen, really wanted to go. Bad. "Daddy, can I go to Jamara's party tonight?"

My father gave Kayren a serious look. He seemed to be considering it. "Will Jamara's parents be there?"

At first, it looked like Kayren was coming up with a plan. But she believed in God and feared to commit a sin. She told the truth. "No, her parents won't be there. They're out of town for the weekend." Knowing he would say no, Kayren put her head down and turned away.

"Kayren, if her parents were going to be there, I wouldn't mind you going, but that's not the case. A lot of bad things can go on if there's not any mature people around to supervise."

With tears in her eyes, Kayren looked back and said, "You don't trust me." She ran into her room and slammed the door.

With a straight face, I looked at my father and said, "She's going to cry about that."

All my father could do was smile. I knew it had to be hard for him, taking care of eight girls and their personalities. So when I could, I tried to assure him that whatever our problem was, we would get over it—and still love him no matter what. Even though we put him through so much, I don't think he ever wanted to trade us in for boys. Not even me.

So he didn't seem to worry much that Kayren didn't come out of her room for the rest of that evening. But then, just before I was supposed to go to bed, the phone rang. While going to answer it, my mom whispered, "I wonder who can be calling at this time of night."

All my father could do was shrug his shoulders.

"Hello . . . . Yes, one second please. Kayren! . . . Kayren!"

Through her door, we heard a faint, "Yes, Mom!"

"Telephone!"

Kayren came out, a surprised look on her face. "Hello? . . . . OK. I will ask him." With a pleading expression on her face, she turned to my father. "Daddy, can I go pick up Kale? He been drinking and can't drive."

My father got that serious look on his face again. "So there was alcohol at the party, huh?" Shaking his head and looking at Mom, he paused for a minute and said, "I guess you can go to pick him up and drop him off to his house. Then come straight back home. Understand?"

"YES! Father, thank you, thank you, thank you!"

"Oh yeah," he added. "You have to take Karma with you."

The look on Kayren's face was part curious, part disappointed. "Karma?"

"Yes, Karma. Karma, honey, go get your jacket. You're riding with your sister."

I couldn't have been more excited as I ran to get my jacket. I'd never been to a high school party before.

Kayren, on the other hand, showed she wasn't too thrilled about taking her little sister to her friend's party. Still, she obeyed our father's orders and were quickly on our way to the party. Now as much as I was glad to be going, I wasn't too thrilled to be picking up Kale. I wouldn't have cared if he drove himself and died in a car accident. OK, I didn't really want him to die. But he could get himself hurt real bad and I wouldn't go visit his selfish ass in the hospital. I really didn't like that dude and I never tried to hide the fact from Kayren. Every time I saw him I mean-mugged the hell outta that punk. He never called me "Karma," which pissed me off. He always had evil names for me, like "Kayren's little demon sister" or "Hellma" instead of "Karma."

"Karma, I know you don't like Kale," Kayren said. I could tell she was about to beg me to be nice to him. "but he is a very kind and passionate man. You just got to get to know him."

Listening to this, for a second I understood Kayren's love for that punk. Daddy always taught me to try to forgive and forget in small situations, but when Kale was around I always had this bad vibe or feeling that he's just an asshole, someone I don't think will ever be on my friends list. Still, until he messed with Kayren, I couldn't do a thing about him. So all I could say was, "Kayren, you're my sister and I love you. Whatever makes you happy will make me happy."

That made Kayren smile. "I love you, too, Karma!" So even though I didn't really mean it, I smiled back. "We're here!"

Already I could see the huge crowd. The place was full of drunken, high and hyped-up high school kids.

Kale was as drunk as any of them. He approached us with an unpleasant greeting. "What the fuck took you so long, Kayren? Oh . . . I see you got Hellma the demon child wit' you. Hey, what's up, Evil—" Kale stuck his hand out to give me a hand shake but I pretended like I was about to bite him. "Little Bitch!" Kale snatched his hand back.

Kayren came to my defense. "Don't ever call her that again, Kale. She is a child. You grow up!"

This tough guy was amazed at Kayren's courage. But he wasn't going to stand for it. He began to pull her out of the car.

"Stop, Kale! You're drunk," Kayren yelled. "You're not in your right state of mind."

Kale kept pulling.

So Kayren finally gave in and got out of the car to avoid another heated scene.

Now at this point, I was already reading Kale's actions and I knew he was going to start some shit. I was right. As soon as Kayren got out of the car, Kale started cussing her out. "Bitch! Who you think you're talking to? Do you know who I am? No one talks to me like that, not even my shit-ass girlfriend! You understand me?"

Kayren didn't answer, just began to walk away.

"Don't you walk away from me!" Then I heard a loud slap. From the car all I could see was Kale pulling his hand back and Kayren falling to the ground. With more force this time, Kale began to go for another slap. Instead, he felt one of my hands blocking his hit and the other hand slapping him to the ground with just as much force as he'd used on Kayren. I could see he was amazed that a six-year-old kid could slap him to the ground. While I was helping Kayren, Kale got back up and tried to sneak me from behind. This is where my years of technique and training paid off. I heard that punk a mile away and ducked, tripping him back to the ground.

My sister yelled, "Please stop, Karma!"

I listened. I knew I could beat him with no problem, so fighting him would be a waste of time. I held back and allowed him to get up again. Even as I was letting him back up, I knew he was going to come back for more. As soon as that thought crossed my mind, here he came swinging, ready for more. Kayren yelled again, "Stop, Kale, before you hurt her!"

Of course he didn't want to listen and still proceeded to swing at me, which was getting him nowhere. Every hit he tried to place on my body missed but got retaliated with a punch to his face. So by the end of the fight, he was bloody up while I was still standing without a scratch. I laughed in his bloody face. "I didn't know my sister was dating a punk-ass football player."

By this time, the whole high school party was watching the action. I was kinda happy to see the attention on us —until he called his homeboys. "What the fuck y'all looking at? Get this kung-fu fighting bitch." His homeboys were smarter than he was. They began to shake their heads and slowly back away like they didn't want any part of it.

I gave Kale a huge smile like, "Yeah, asshole, your own friends don't want no part of this."

That just pissed Kale off to the limits. Next thing I know, this punk-ass is pulling out a knife. That instantly turned me from playful fighting mode to serious danger mode.

"Kale, what the fuck are you doing?" Kayren screamed.

"Stay out of this, Kayren!" he hollered back.

I whispered, "Back up, Kayren. Let him go."

With all the force he had left, Kale came charging towards me with the knife. I instantly slapped it out of his hand, tripped him and started beating his ass. Not just because he'd threatened my life, but my sister's as well. I whipped his ass for a good long time; seemed like fifteen minutes to me, but probably wasn't but one or two. Finally, Kayren begged me to stop. I stood up to a crowd of stunned, scared and speechless. I don't know which shocked them more: that a girl had whipped his ass or that it was a six-year-old. Either way, they were surprised. And they knew that this six-year-old girl had just whipped a seventeen-year-old all-star football player's ass without getting a scratch.

"Karma, get in the car!" I obeyed Kayren and quickly jumped in. On the way home there was nothing but silence. I could tell Kayren was shocked that her little sister had strength like that. About a block away from home, Kayren couldn't help herself but to speak about what had just happened, but not in the way I expected. "Karma, please don't tell Daddy what happened. Kale is a great person; he just has his ways like everyone else."

All I could do was shake my head and keep quiet. But once we pulled up in the driveway, I looked at my sister and whispered, "I'll keep this a secret if you promise that next time he fuck wit' you I can kill him."

Kayren started laughing at me until she looked over to see just how serious her little sister's face was. She didn't laugh any more after that.

Daddy greeted us with a smile. "Hello girls! Was the party a state away?"

"No, Daddy," Kayren said. "I haven't been to Jamara's in a long time and I got lost!"

"Well, next time, at least call me. Now go to sleep and get ya'll some rest."

Kayren and I rushed to our rooms before he could ask any more questions. As I got to my room, I felt a hug from behind. "Thanks, Karma for keeping this a secret for me." She knew that this was a huge deal for me, because I never keep secrets. Especially from my father. What she said next gave me such a thrill I didn't worry about the secret anymore. She said I could kill Kale if he messed with her again. So that's what I was going to do!

While lying in my bed, thinking it all over, I did feel a bit of guilt about not telling my father. So I decided that tomorrow I'd tell him what happened.

But the doorbell got to him before I did. From my bedroom, I could hear what he was saying. "Hello, officers. What brings you to my home this time of night?"

"Well, we're looking for a suspect who apparently assaulted a young man tonight at a party on Malibu Avenue."

"Really? I'm surprised you're looking for your subject in this neighborhood, let alone at my home," he told the cops. "Well, I'm sorry, officer, but I can't help you with that matter."

The cop answered, "I'm sorry, sir, but one of the suspects' name is Karma Commander. We understand that she resides here. Is that true?"

A long pause told me Daddy was figuring things out. "Yes, sir. She's my daughter." Forcefully, he called for me. "Karma Commander, come downstairs. Now."

As soon as I knew the police were there I started feeling nervous. Not because I'd defended my sister, but that I hadn't told my father. I already knew he would to be disappointed that I'd kept a secret from him. When I got to the front door, I saw two cops; their mouths hung open when they got a look at me. The one whose voice I'd heard from my room coughed and asked, "Is this Karma?"

I could hear the relief in my father's voice. "Yes, sir. This is my six-year-old daughter, Karma Commander. So as you see, you must have the wrong person."

The cop looked at my father, then at Kayren, who had showed up when she heard the conversation. He kneeled down, looked at me and asked, "Karma, were you at a party tonight on Malibu Avenue?" I looked at my father.

"Be completely honest, Karma."

"Yes, sir. I was there, riding with my sister. But only for a brief moment."

"Well, a high school student and a few other witnesses say you attacked him when he was in a dispute with your older sister, Kayren." He looked up at Kayren, who avoided making eye contact. "Is that true?"

I paused for a minute, thinking how Kale was a snitch and a coward for telling on me to the cops. "Yes, sir, I did. But he'd hit my sister. I was trying to defend her. I didn't mean to hurt him until he pulled out a knife."

"I didn't hear anything about a knife," the cop said. "All I know is that this young man is in the hospital getting treatment, including stitches, for injuries he say you committed."

"He did have a knife. I promise."

Kayren kneeled down beside me and finally looked directly at the cop. "Yes, officer, he did. I was there."

The officer paused for another brief moment. He stood up and looked at his partner before speaking. "Well, considering what you said about a weapon, we're not prepared to press any charges at this time." The other cop nodded. "We'll be interviewing the young man again before we wrap up this case," the first cop continued. Turning to my father, now, he said, "You understand, sir that we had to investigate this and talk with you all. We want to be sure this situation won't happen again."

"It won't, officer," I told him. "Unless he attacks my sister again and ya'll aren't around to help her."

Both cops chuckled. "Understood, Ms. Karma Commander," said the one who'd done all the talking. "Off the record, I would have done the same." The police officer gave me a wink. He turned to speak to my father. "You have a little killer on your hands, huh? Ha, ha, ha. Y'all folks have a good night."

As soon as the door shut behind the officers, I turned to go back to my room, like, "OK, glad that's over," until I heard Daddy.

"Wait a minute, Karma. You're not getting off that easy. Now why didn't you tell me about this?"

"I was going to tell you," I said, "but I was just waiting till tomorrow."

"Don't you think this was important enough to tell me tonight?"

"Yes, sir. But I promised Kayren!"

"Oh, the plot thickens." I couldn't be sure if he was mad, or thought this was funny. Maybe some of both. "Kayren asked you not to tell me, huh?"

"Yes, sir. And I agreed. I have no excuse and I should be punished." I lowered my head, waiting for his answer.

When it came, my father spoke with authority. "Karma. Never lower your head in shame for anything you do. You must learn that whatever you do, you must know the consequences beforehand. If you're still determined, then complete your mission and have no regrets. As far as tonight is concerned, you were not wrong for defending your sister and yourself but you were wrong for keeping it discreet from me. I'm your father and I know what's best for you. Understand?"

I looked him in the eye. "Yes, sir."

"OK. Now go and run fifteen laps for your punishment."

"Yes, sir." I ran to put on my running gear on and started out the door.

"Karma! One other thing. While you're running, I want you to think about what I just told you about no regrets. When you come back, I want you to give me your true thought about regrets. Understood?" The cool breeze felt nice as I started my run. It only took me an hour; I ran much farther than that every day anyway. It was still dark when I got home but I came in to find my father cooking breakfast.

"Hello, Karma. I've been waiting for you. Should have taken less than an hour." There he went again, pushing me to become better.

"I know. I'm sorry. Next time it will be forty-five minutes. Promise!"

"Sit down, Karma, and eat your breakfast. You know I don't mean to push you too hard but I see so much potential in you. I can see you becoming the best our ancestors ever created, and I'm not saying this because you're my daughter."

"I understand, Daddy, but I have so many questions. I don't understand why I'm so different. I asked Kayla how many weapons she has and she said, 'None.' Why am I practicing with knives, guns and other deadly weapons when my sisters are playing with Barbie dolls and other toys? Kids get to play every day but I just get to play for a few hours on the weekends. And why don't my sisters get trained like me?" I looked at him, hoping for answers.

All he could do was wait silently. It seemed like forever. Then he looked at me and said, "Do you trust God?"

"Yes."

"Do you trust me?"

"Yes."

"Well, while you're trusting, you will have to listen to what I'm about to tell you and take it to your peaceful grave. No one must know. Not your sisters, nor your mother, your friends, et cetera. No one! The ones who know will not discuss this with you, because you aren't supposed to know this until you're ten. But like I said before, you are different from any one of us."

Now I was more confused than ever. I finished the last sausage on my plate and gave my father my full attention. I knew by the look on his face that this going to be some serious shit.

Chapter 7

Born to kill

My father took a big sip of his coffee, took a deep breath and began to prepare himself for a long talk. "Karma, you're a huge part of an obligation that's been going on for years to serve our God. Me, your grandmother, your great-grandfather, going all the way back to his great-grandfather, all played a huge part in making this obligation successful. We, as a family, have to continue this circle of life so we can make the world a better place."

"How can we make the world a better place, Daddy?"

His answer was what I'd been waiting for as long as I could remember.

"By killing a lot of the bad ones in the world, Karma." Those words scared me, but then I started to get excited, too. "You see, there are many people that live secret lives and hide them so well the police can't catch them. But we can. We can make a difference by finding the ones that have committed inhuman crimes and finish them."

"But Daddy, isn't that a sin? Christian and I been learning about that, a little."

"Yes, Karma, it is a sin, but that's how the world is and we are killing for right reasons. We're no different from the police officers who shoot drug dealers or the judges that sentence convicts to death."

"We not different?"

"Yes, we are different from them, but we are also much the same. We both want justice but we just go by it in a different way. We confide in God's workers, who are Steven and Christian. They know who is good and who is bad by listening to so many people confessing their sins in the confession booth. They try hard to help them change their lives, but if they don't, that's where we come in. We come in and destroy them. In time you will understand the Bible more and all these things will make sense. Christian is studying hard, learning the Bible day by day, so he can teach you the rights and wrongs of life. Remember everything Christian teaches you and everything he preaches to you from the Bible, for that is how you find peace with God. Christian is teaching you just like Steven taught me, his grandfather taught my grandfather, and so on. All these things you will learn from him are what have been taught to us for centuries."

With all that had been said, I was completely in shock. All I could say was, "It's time for me to truly understand."

My father replied, "In time you will. First you must get to know God better, before you learn death. So while your training will focus on learning, as far as life is concerned you must always keep God in your mind and heart. Time will tell all." Then he gave me a harder look. "And maybe, just maybe, you will stop all this cussing."

I didn't stop the cussing. But I did learn and trained more. By the time I was twelve, still with no tears in my eyes, I'd improved my physical abilities by massive training, improved my learning skills, and last but most important, improved my relationship with God and with Christian. Every day, we were reading the Bible together and he was teaching me everything I ever needed to know about God. I even cut back, some, on the cussing. Every single lesson I had with Christian was a lovely experience but one particular lesson is what changed my life forever.

We usually met at the park but this time Christian wanted to do something different and learn at the beach. I agreed and was there on time, like usual, but for the first time Christian was late. "Wow, Christian, the end must be near if you're late. It's the first time since I met you."

Christian gave me a reassuring smile. "I was talking to my father. He kept drilling today's lesson into my head. Guess he's scared I'll get something wrong."

"Well, I'm ready. Because this must be extra important for you to be late and all." I guess I was a little nervous; I covered it up with a laugh.

"It is extra important, Karma. Today's lesson is one of the most important I will ever teach you."

I could tell this was major because even though Christian and I were both twelve, he was very mature and completely serious when it came to our lessons. Nervous as I was, I could tell he had confidence in his lesson he was about to teach. He took a breath of relief and began. "Back in the eighteen hundreds there was a man name Caesar who talked to God on a day-to-day basis. He ate, slept and lived by God. Anything God needed, he was there, no matter what it was. God always asked him to do things on Earth to keep it safer from the secretly deceitful people. Of course, Caesar agreed and obeyed God's every command and never questioned it, until one day God asked him to kill a man named Bishop. Caesar began to cry and doubt his communication with God. He thought maybe he was going crazy, that maybe it was his own mind putting voices in his head instead of God. So for the first time ever in his life he questioned God. He asked, 'In the Bible it says, "Thou shalt not kill." Why would you ask me to do such a thing?' God replied, 'There are people who kill many of my children day by day and shouldn't live on earth.' Caesar then asked God, 'Please show me a sign that I'm talking to you and not the voices in my head.' Without hesitation, God made a light bulb glow that was not attached to anything electrical. And then he said, 'Whenever you come to this spot, you will see this light bulb glow for eternity. Your grandchildren and their grandchildren will always have this light bulb to show I've been here and that the missions they are sent to do are sent by me. On the precise day, I will send you someone who has gone through exactly what you have. Y'all will meet up and know exactly what to do.' With tears of confidence, Caesar completed his mission. And just like God said, he found his best friend, with the same experiences. Karma, do you know what this friend's his name is?"

"No."

"His name was Karman Commander. Your great-great-great grandfather."

When I heard this, I paused for a minute and thought about my father and the things he'd told me when I was six. "So are you saying that God sends us on missions to kill people who had done terrible crimes?"

"Yes but he only talks to us. And when I say 'us,' I'm referring to my father and me. You see, Karma, my bloodline was made to talk to God; yours was made to complete God's mission. Together, we're the middle, the world between good and evil."

I finally found the words to ask him a question. "Why did God choose your family to talk to him and ours to kill for him?"

It's like he was expecting the question. Quickly, Christian answered. "When God talked to our great-great grandfathers on the same day it was a test, not of who was the best one to serve him but who was the best in the certain type of duty that needed to be fulfilled. Either way, to do the things we've done, we both have to have faith in him. On that particular day, my ancestor chose to talk to God again before he committed a murder; your ancestor chose to kill as soon as he got God's command. Both acted with the same faith and trust; just one chose to ask and one didn't."

"So you're saying that just by one action God knew which was the one who should talk to him?"

"Karma, look a little deeper. God chose your family to kill because your blood had no fear of doing so, as long as y'all knew God was asking. But as far as us, we couldn't trust our own mind, so in time it would be hard to trust another person's word. Your ancestors, through the centuries, had so much faith that you didn't have to question. As long as it was God's word than you would do it. It takes a lot of strength and belief to kill another person and still sleep at night."

Through the lesson, I was mostly silent, but by the time he said this, I was completely lost for words.

I just shook my head a little, my mouth hanging open. I guess he could tell that was all I could think about for a while.

"I think that's enough for tonight, Karma."

"I agree." I gave him a smile started to walk back home. I was still a little confused but also confident that I could live up to this.

"Karma," Christian called after me. "If you're still having doubts, I want you to take a look at this." I'd already gotten ten steps away from him when I turned around, and that's when I first saw a glow that I'd never seen before. In Christian's hands was an old-fashioned light bulb. It looked so old it looked like it had no possible way working, even with electricity. And let alone working without it. But there it was, in his hands, without a wire in sight, glowing with a shine I couldn't describe if I had a lifetime to think about it. All I could do was stare in amazement.

I knew then that what Christian had been saying was true. I could feel it in my heart: I was born to kill.

When I got back home I was silent for a while. I couldn't confide in my sisters, so I went to my room until dinner time. As usual, Mom called out, "Kids! Time for dinner!" But then she stuck her head in my door and said, quietly, "Karma, your father wants you to meet him in the quiet room for dinner."

I already knew he knew what Christian had told me "Hey, Daddy." I came into the quiet room and sat down.

"Hello, Karma. I know that with all you heard today that you'd need some peace and quiet, so I decided to have dinner with you in here."

I looked at him and nodded, not speaking.

"Think about what Christian has told you; because everything he has said, to the last word, is completely true. All the questions you have with me will be answered tomorrow. As far as tonight . . . Just enjoy the silence, but give it all thought."

I obeyed my father and said nothing about what Christian and I had talked about. All that night I couldn't sleep, just kept thinking about my father and what I had just learned about our family history.

First thing the next morning, I was up and dressed for training ten minutes early. I was more than anxious to add the missing pieces to the story. I knew that only my father could tell me.

"Good morning, Karma," he greeted me in the kitchen. "How did you sleep?"

"I slept OK, but not as usual."

"I understand that. You had a lot to bear after just taking in all that information."

"Speaking of that, Daddy, I have a lot of unanswered questions. Before I completely understand what I was born to do, I have to have them answered."

I could see the strong sympathy in my father's eyes. "Karma, all your questions have been answered. You're just trying to figure out if the answers are true or not. I know everything is confusing and hard to accept all at once. But Karma, you are a killer. You were born to kill. Have you ever wondered why you don't have the ability to cry? It's because you were born with no fear or passion to bring about a crying emotion. Have you ever wondered why you love to train? Why you have the heart to practice with lethal weapons and have no doubt that you're the best? That's because you are the best, and deep down inside you know this. You always knew. You may think you're surprised that you were born to kill. But deep down inside, you already know what you're on earth to do. Now you must accept."

I turned and look at my father, filled with confidence. "You're right! I always knew I was special; I just couldn't figure out for what. But I get it. I was born to kill."

"Yes, Karma. Yes you were!"

After that it was on. I was no longer just training; I was training to kill, all day and night. Except during school hours. By now I was running ten miles a day nonstop, swimming twenty laps a day, doing three hundred pull-ups then three hundred pushups, and learning my ninja and kung-fu skills to perfection. I was also working on my silent skills in the quiet room. I was at the peak of my training, not just for the future but for my very first mission. That would be in just a month, on my thirteenth birthday.

To help make sure I wouldn't have any doubts about my first mission, my father told me to go see Steven. I ran all the way to his church, where he was waiting for me.

"Karma, I wanted to explain a little more just how important you are to the world and how your obligations are so completely justified. I know you have been studying your Old Testament; isn't that right?"

I nodded. He got reports about our Bible study from Christian every day.

"In Joshua 6:21 to 25," Steven said, "God orders that every living thing in the city of Jericho must be killed. And in the New Testament, Hebrews 10:28 states that anyone who rejected the law of Moses died without mercy."

I remembered studying both those verses. "Do you know why this happened?"

"No, sir, I don't."

"It happened, Karma, because it was a must! These people who were put to death refused to obey God's law. They didn't want to change, so they had to be destroyed. You will give justice just like Moses had to. You will only kill when it's a necessity and for the right reasons; your one killing will help save many other people."

I knew all that. I had heard it from my father, from Christian, and from Steven, too. But I still wondered how many chances even a bad person should get.

It's like Steven guessed what I was thinking. "Karma, I try my best to change these people that are causing destruction around the world, but when I can't, I must send your father—or you—to destroy them.

"Yes, killing is a sin. But it's also forgiven when it's done for the right reasons. Kinda like if you killed someone that was trying to kill you. You wouldn't go to jail because it's self-defense. America has its laws about what is right and what is wrong and when a killing is justified. And so does the Bible, Karma. Even though America wouldn't understand that what we're doing is right, just know that we are right. And we must continue to do this to make the world a better place. Unfortunately, we must not tell anyone we do so. People didn't understand Jesus and he was put to death; so even though we are completely good in all that we do, we must keep it a secret. Karma, we must trust in each other, just as we do in God and in the Bible."

I thought about this for a minute as Steven waited patiently. "I understand, Mr. Steven."

After that important Bible lesson, I was quickly back home and back to my training.

While my father was training me, he had a mission of his own to prepare. Through my nine years of growing up, my father had been preparing for a very special kill of his own. I knew something was up because he was going to another church during the week; we were only going to Steven's church on Sundays. I didn't know exactly what was going on but I could feel it in my father's soul. He was working on something big.

"Daddy, can I go with you today when you go see Mr. Steven?"

"No, Karma. I would love to take you but you're not the right age yet. You will be soon!" My father kissed me on my forehead before he left.

"Love you, Daddy!" I called after him.

"Love you too, Karma.". I never knew exactly what my father and Steven had their meetings about, but I did know that every single one of them was important. I knew he took every single one of them seriously.

~

Steven never knew this, but whenever my father went into the confessional, he secretly recorded their conversations. It wasn't that he didn't trust Steven, but he thought that some day it would help me to hear what they talked about. He was right, of course. But he had no idea just how much those tapes would help me. When I found them, much later, this is what the first one sounded like.

"Forgive me, Father for I have sinned . . . ."

"Hello, Sincere! How is Karma?"

"She is doing very well. She is training better than any killer I've ever seen, including myself."

"Really? That's funny, because Christian says she's in the top five with him in high school academics. She's just smart all around, huh?"

"Yes, Steven, she is."

"Do you think she's ready?"

"Yes I do. To be honest, I think she's been ready since she turned nine. She's so much more advanced that it's hard for me to keep up at times. She's now capable of running a half marathon in an hour and a quarter; she swims like a thieving fish; and she can shoot on a target from a one-mile range with the right gun. She is already so advanced for her age, and she's still got so much time."

"That's great news, Sincere. It brings me great relief that the tradition will continue for another lifetime. Now how about you? Are you ready to complete this mission?"

"Yes, I'm ready. I just have some concerns. I've been going to Pastor Carson's church like you told me. I've been there hours out of every day volunteering and even became a member just like you wanted me to. But I don't know if I can kill him like you want me too."

Steven answered calmly but his frustration showed in his voice. "With all our past, you're going to just question our actions? And why now?"

"I studied his every move. Where he ate, where he slept and the type of family man he was. For nine years. I don't think I can just kill him without knowing exactly why."

"Sincere! Don't you trust me? Don't you trust God?"

"Yes, but—"

"No buts. Just a yes or a no answer."

"Yes."

"OK. Well, I expect him to be dead soon."

"OK. Done." After the meeting, he was feeling all types of ways. He couldn't kick the feeling he had about killing this man he felt was innocent.

This Pastor Carson is a great family man, Sincere believed. He studies the Bible like it's his life, and he gives to the community every day. The reason for this mission must be something more and he only had a month to figure it out.

So for a whole month, as my father was preparing me for my kill, he was researching his own kill as well.

~

A month before my birthday, I finally found out what my first mission was going to be. His name was Mikael. He was sixteen, a pretty-boy type with a mother who's a doctor and a father who's a lawyer. What was going to make him a dead man was that he bullied a lot of kids at his school. His bullying caused six of them to commit suicide. On top of that, he raped two of his classmates. None of his actions were ever acknowledged because his mother and father had paid off the victims' families. But now it's time for their precious son to pay. I didn't have to do much to get to know him. All I had to do was dress cute and chill at the park where he usually met his ignorant friends.

"Damn! You fine!"

Bingo! I looked to my left to see the one and only Mikael Madders. Which name fit him so good, due to the fact he thought he mattered to everybody.

"Hello, Mikael. I'm Charlie! I just moved up the street."

"How you know my name?"

"I hear all the talk about how fine you are."

Confidently, Mikael replied, "I bet they do, baby! All of them want me, but since you're new, I'll let you get the first try."

"First try, huh? Well! I'm more than honored." The first week, I got to know him very well. We played video games, we ran together, we tutored each other and all.

He was feeling so comfortable with me that he opened up about something important. "Karma, I need to tell you something. You know how my father is such a big shot, right?"

I nodded.

"Well, everybody thinks he's such a great family man. But he's not! I found out he was cheating on my mom. He started having sex with another woman, and she even had babies with him! I hate him so much for what he's done to my mother."

"That's terrible," I said.

"It's not right that he can get away with that, is it?" he said.

"No, it's not right," I agreed.

"I think any man who does that deserves to be punished," Mikael went on. "Along with any woman he's cheating with. Especially the woman. She's the one breaking up a happy home, right?"

"Yeah, I guess so," I said. Whether I'd agreed with him or not, I'd have pretended that I did, just to get him to trust me. But about this, I did agree. So for the first time in my mission, I didn't have to lie. "Sure. They both ought to pay."

After that, Mikael even admitted, for a second, that he was starting to feel he was in love. Ha. It was that Karma swag that Charlie was putting out. Either way, I didn't feel any love for him. I was just ready to kill, and I was only three days away from doing so.

My father was on point with the days till my kill, too. "Karma, your big day is coming up. Are you excited, nervous or scared?"

"No, Daddy. None of the above. I'm just ready. I think after my first kill I will feel better."

"Karma, you are just like I was when I was waiting on my first kill."

"How old were you?"

"Same age. We all committed our first kill at thirteen. You always remember your first kill, even after you've killed thirty or more. My first was an eighty eight year old fisherman; he'd been part of the Holocaust. He'd helped murder over seven hundred innocent people in the past."

"We kill people 'cause of the past, too?"

"Not unless the past is still relevant. Mr. Retired Fisherman was still killing people from time to time, hiding their bodies under water. So at thirteen I was sent to kill him. I must admit I was very nervous but while underwater in my mission to kill him I came across the bodies of half a dozen people he'd killed recently: men, woman and children. At that point I realized that my one murder would save many murders. Karma, once you realize this, you will become more at peace within yourself."

"I think I'm almost there, Daddy."

"Get some rest, Karma. You have a lot to prepare for." He was right; I was about to prepare for one of the biggest days of my life. It was time to get ready, but I still had two days until my kill. So I still had to stay as close to Mikael as possible. He began to truly fall in love with "Charlie." Well, so he thought. I was just playing the role of what I knew he would like. He loved sports; so did I. He loved race cars; so did I. He also loved me. Ha! So did I. I even accepted some of his nasty dark secrets. I kept telling him I agreed with him about being mad at his father and at his father's mistress. I wanted him to trust me more than he could trust anyone. It was on the second day before his death that he showed me the reason why I was killing him.

"Charlie, can I show you something?"

"Sure you can, boo, show me anything you want."

"Well, let's take a walk." Mikael took my hand and began to lead me down a dirt road with lots of beautiful trees and bushes full of flowers. I knew he was taking me somewhere special.

But the farther we walked, the wilder it got. We went from gorgeous flowers to what I could tell was leading into deep, shaded woods. It was all trees, bushes, with a flower here and there, where they were lucky to get just enough sun to bloom. Straight ahead, this dirt trail was leading to Mikael's deep dark secrets. After twenty minutes we got to his secret spot. The trail ended at an old shed, covered with vines and almost hidden behind bushes and trees. Completely unnoticeable, even to a hunter's eye. "This is my dad's old hunting camp," Mikael said. "But he doesn't hunt anymore. He quit coming out here, so now I have it all to myself."

And now I had him all to myself.

"Charlie, you're the reason why we're here. Because I'm about to show you something I've never showed anyone. I feel that we connect in so many ways. One of them is how we both hate fathers who cheat on their wives. We hate how they can go out and have sex with a woman and make a child outside their happy home. We both agree that people should pay; right?"

In my mind, I was saying, again, He has a point, I guess. So just for this, out of everything else I'd done in my mission, I was honest with him. "Yes, I feel like they should pay. The husbands that comment adultery should spend some time in jail, especially if a baby is involved."

Mikael lowered his head and shook it slowly. Then I realized exactly who

I was dealing with. So my next comment was, "Matter of fact, they should die! How dare they ruin a happy home?"

Mikael instantly lifted his head with a huge smile. I knew then that I had him right in the palms of my hands. "Karma . . . It's that time." Mikael went to the shed, pushed away some vines, and slowly opened the door. Inside, lined up on the floor, were three human heads! A woman's and two children. Looked like a girl, about three years old, and a baby boy. My heart started beating fast. I was thinking, This sick freak is going around killing women and children and keeping their heads as a memory. My training paid off, though. As far as Mikael could see, I was calm and happy. I spoke to him like I was impressed. "True brilliance, Mikael; true brilliance. Why didn't I think of that? To kill the mistress so she wouldn't mess up a happy home."

With an even bigger smile, Mikael whispered, "I didn't just kill my father's mistress. I also got her kids, too!"

I slowly turned to look at Mikael and asked him, reassuringly, "Her kids, too?"

"Hell, yeah! My father cheated on my mother and got the bitch pregnant. I had to watch my mother cry every day for months just because my father betrayed her. They still together, but that's because his mistress quit returning his calls and wouldn't answer the door. He didn't know why, but it's 'cause I killed her and her babies, too!"

Now I'd been trained to kill without question, because Daddy and Steven promised that my targets would deserve it. But now I was hearing Mikael talking the same way. Except for him it was more than just duty. No, he enjoyed this!

"So now I'm gonna find more of these bitches and give them what they deserve," he went on. "I'm gonna kill every woman that think she can just ruin a marriage."

I kept that admiring smile on my face, but deep inside I was feeling so much anger. He thought he had a right to kill innocent people just because they were having sex and getting caught up. His morals are completely screwed up. I knew then, for myself, that he must die!

After his tour around his room of death, we walked back to the park. I was mostly quiet, letting Mikael do all the talking on the way back. All I could do was think of how I was going to kill him. My father once told me that we all have our own way of killing people so we could set our minds at peace and that one day I will know mine. At the time he told me, I didn't know exactly how I could just know how to kill someone and feel at peace with it. Not till today. Not till right now, as we spoke at this park. Mikael, with that look of love in his eyes like always, wanted the last word. "Karma, I love you! You're all I need to complete my triangle of love and hate."

As I turned to leave, I replied, "I Love you, too, Mikael! See you tomorrow."

While walking home, all I could see was me killing Mikael but, to give him credit, I kind of understood the way he felt about committing adultery. But he doesn't have the right to kill! Still, he does have the right to ask for forgiveness. I feel we all do.

Finally it was time to kill this bastard. So early the next morning, I set up my gear, got my school work and headed off to school to begin my mission.

"Hey, Karma! Wait!" my father yelled from the door. "Did you get every-thing you need for your special day today?"

"Yes, Daddy, I did."

"OK. great! I expect you home by seven. OK?" I knew my father was ner-vous about this being my first mission and all, but on the other hand, he was also excited. It was my first try-out for my career. I had a lot of mixed feelings about the mission. Even though Mikael was already a serial killer, I also saw a kind side to him. Maybe, I told myself, he was a kid who had been living good but got caught up in his parents' mess, which is why he'd started killing. By now, I truly get how I'd be killing him because of my parents' history. So maybe, just maybe, I could help before I killed.

Like always, soon as school was out I was at the park to meet Mikael. Like always, he was on time and ready to see his lovely lady. While greeting me with a hug, Mikael whispered, "I've been thinking about you all day! I missed you." I knew after he told me his secrets and I accepted them that he was go-ing to love me more but this was beyond my imagination. He didn't let go, but hugged me for like two or three minutes, as if he'd thought I wasn't going to show up.

All I could do was gaze into his eyes and smile back as if I loved him the same or even more. "Mikael, can you take me to your special place? I would love to add to your collection!"

He stared back into my eyes; with tears in his eyes. "I'm way ahead of you." He took my hand and led me to the street where an old camper was parked. He pulled a key out of his pocket and unlocked the side door. "Charlie, it's time to put our love to the test." Mikael opened the door and there in the camper lay a woman and a little boy, tied up, with rags over their faces.

I began to smile. I wanted him to think I was happy and excited that he had innocent people in his truck, scared for their lives.

"Come on, Charlie. Let's go." We got in the truck and he drove it down the long dirt road to Mikael's special spot." While driving, all he could talk about was how he'd been able to catch this new mother and her child.

All I could think about was how I was going to kill him. I hadn't planned to have innocent people involved in this, but it was cool. I had my plan.

Finally we got to his shack, where he got out and went around to the camper's side door. "Charlie, this is about to be one of the best days of your—"

I knocked him in the head with my .45. He fell to the ground, passed out. I quickly tied him up, found the keys in his pocket and opened his shed. Inside was a chair; I dragged it out and propped him up in it. In a couple of minutes he started to come to.

"Hello, Mikael. I see you've awakened."

Tears of anger in his eyes, he shouted, "What the fuck, Charlie! Why are you doing this to me?

I kept my voice calm and settled. "My name is Karma, not Charlie, and for weeks I've been planning to kill you. You have become a sick boy, Mikael, and your only cure is death. You've already killed a woman and her children and I can see you plan to keep doing it."

By this time the tears were streaming down Mikael's face. "When I get loose," he screamed, "I'm going to kill you!"

I gave him a slim smile at this. Then I cocked my hand back and placed a huge slap on his face to show him I meant business. "Mikael. You have killed an innocent woman and children, and plan to kill more, just because your father was a man who couldn't keep his penis in his pants. But you're no better than he is! You're a terrible man. You should believe a sin is a sin; their sins are no better or worst then your sins.

"Tonight you have two ways you can die. Confess your sins and ask for forgiveness then die at peace with God. Or die as a man who hasn't felt any guilt for his sins."

"Bitch!" I could hear evil in Mikael's voice. "You don't know my pain. They deserved it. These women that don't have a life and the only job they have is to fuck up other people's lives; they all deserve to die."

I began to see where this was going. I wanted him to hear that I was sincere. "Mikael, remember: they might have taken a few moments of happiness, but you can get that back. But if you take a life away, they can never come back." I pointed to the shed where his first victims were, and to the camper where the next ones waited. "Mikael, think about the mothers and fathers of these women; about the grandparents of these children. Do you feel their pain?"

"Yes, girl, I do. And that is what makes my heart high! I feel better knowing that people are crying and feeling pain like I did when my father hurt my mother! You know what, Karma or whatever the fuck your name is? I feed off their pain!" He nodded toward the shed. "I went to that bitch's funeral, just so I could see her family mourn. And then I went to the cemetery and spit on their graves." As his rant went on, the tears were streaming down his face. "You think because you have me tied up that I was going to change? Bitch, please! If I die today, I'll die a happy soul!"

I whispered, "Mikael, you have no soul."

With the silencer on my .45, I shot him, close range to the head.

I had tried to help before I hurt; I had failed. Still, I told myself, I won't give up. From now on, I will give a chance before I kill.

After I made sure Mikael was dead, I changed into an all-black outfit and covered my face and hair. I also put on taller boots to change my height, then unlocked the camper and untied Mikael's next intended victims. The woman was too terrified to speak, which was fine with me. I didn't want her to hear my voice. I handed her the cell phone Mikael had taken from her and disappeared. From a distance, I watched the police come rescue the woman and child, put on my running gear and headed on home.

While running home, all that entered my mind was how much anger Mikael had inside. I asked myself if I had let him live, would it have changed him? The answer to that question I will never know.

Ten miles later I was back home, ready for dinner. The family was already waiting for me. I was literally running late. Of course, Santana had something to say. "Karma, where have you been? You need to be on time like everyone else. You're not special."

"Shut up, Santana!"

My father shook his head. "Karma, how was school?"

"It went perfect, Daddy."

With a huge smile, my father continued eating.

Chapter 8

Knowing truth with fear.

After my first kill I was completing six-month missions and training harder than I'd ever trained in my life. I was mastering more advanced assassin techniques and doing more and harder work than a twenty-year veteran. Steven told my father I was the best assassin in history and I was only twelve years old. I knew I was special because the missions I'd completed had been no problem. Just to name a few, I'd killed five kids who were known to be serial killers. One kid was going around killing old people because he felt like they were a waste of space. Another one killed teachers because he'd had to repeat the ninth grade. All the kids I've killed were too full of their killing ways; so full they wouldn't be able to turn back.

Before I completed my first kill, my father told me I was going to have to come up with something that would set my mind at peace afterwards. So I decided to give each of my victims the chance to ask for forgiveness before they died, and if I deeply felt they could change, that maybe, just maybe, I would let them go. Still, even with much hope, it doesn't look like it will be happening anytime soon.

My missions were on completely sick kids my age who really didn't want to change; they justified their actions. So at that point it was ten killed, zero saved.

My father was so proud of me. I was twelve, making straight A's in the ninth grade while playing varsity basketball. I also was reading the Bible every day. At this point in my life, I was quoting verses from memory only and trying my best to follow the Bible as much as possible. Even though I had many sins on me I still had strong beliefs in the Bible and God. I loved him more than I loved myself, which was why I had no regrets at all about committing my killings. I knew my instructions were from God so it was real. Everything was going perfectly.

Until three days before my thirteenth birthday. My father called me into the quiet room. I knew it was something important, like another mission, because today was not the day to practice Ninja fighting.

"Have a seat, Karma; I would like to discuss something with you. First off, how does it feel to know you're the best killer in the world at the age of twelve? With over ten kills?"

I looked up at my father with a humble smile. "It feels great. Especially doing it for God!"

With those small words alone I could tell that it filled a special place in his heart. He smiled and said, "You see! Right there! You're always adding God in everything you do, which is great! I truly admire that. I see you've found peace within yourself. So now I must ask: how do you kill and then set your mind at peace?"

At first it was hard for me to give an answer in words; then suddenly they came out. "I allow them to ask for forgiveness and let them make the decision. Knowing that I gave them the opportunity to set their minds at peace allows me to set my mind at peace."

For a second my father looked at me with amazement. "Karma, do you believe that everything happens for a reason?"

"Yes, Daddy, I do."

He reached out and gave me a huge hug. "Karma, I have a mission that I have to complete soon. Of all my missions, I'm thinking the hardest about this one. So if you don't mind, I'm going to try your way at setting my mind at peace." My father then winked as if there should not be any concern. "I'm proud of you, Karma! I'm looking forward to watching you grow and having kids of your own."

I put on my ill face and said, "Kids? Gross!"

He began to laugh. "Good night, Karma."

"Goodnight, Daddy . . . . Hey, Daddy. Before tonight, how did you set your mind at peace?"

"Well, Karma, I was just asking myself the same question." My father seemed to have a lot on his mind but I brushed it off, 'cause if I didn't know everything about him I did know he was a strong man who can handle anything.

~

The next day it was time for my father to go talk to Pastor Steven, like usual, with his mini recorder hidden in his jacket.

"Father, forgive me, for I have sinned. It's been exactly a month today since my last confession and I'm still feeling a little discomfort about killing this man. He seems like he hasn't done anything wrong. He only preaches the word of God."

"Sincere, I thought we discussed this and that you were ready to complete it. He may speak the word of God but God wants him dead," Steven said, softly, "and that is your mission."

"But—"

"No 'buts,' Sincere!" His voice had turned harsh.

Obediently, Sincere replied, "Yes, sir" and turned to leave the confessional.

"Sincere," Steven said, "remember that only you have the power to complete God's mission. Your blood line was chosen. So no matter how hard the mission may be, you have to look beyond yourself."

With an uneasy smile, Sincere replied, "Yes, I understand, Steven. I love God and I will do anything for him." The smile on his face hid what he was really feeling. Even though Sincere was confident in God, and since he was a child he'd been taught to obey Steven's commands, he felt like it would be wrong to complete this mission by killing a preacher who had not done wrong.

He knew he had to come up with a plan to give himself a little more time. So for hours he rode the streets of our Florida town, deep into his thoughts. He didn't end up at home until three in the morning. I was still up. My father had trained me so well and I've always been around him so I couldn't sleep until he got home. My mother had told me earlier to go to bed, but I still couldn't. I camouflaged myself behind the furniture and waited silently without her noticing. My training was so perfect to the point that I was almost in my mother's face without her knowing it or hearing even a breath.

As soon as I heard the key turn and my father enter, I was excited and happy to see him. Still, I wanted to see if he could tell I was in the room, so I stayed quiet. My mother, of course, greeted him with a huge hug and a question I didn't understand. "How'd it go?" Those three words gave me a little concern because I knew he'd gone to see Pastor Steven, and after those visits my mother never questioned anything.

But tonight was different. Instead of answering the question, he replied, "Are all the girls asleep?"

"Yes, Baby, they are. I made Karma go to sleep as well."

He turned with a smile. "Well, you think you put Karma to sleep, but really she's right there." My father pointed to the book shelf.

I could see the confusion on her face. "Sincere, there are nothing but books over there."

He spoke confidently, "Karma, you can come out now."

I began to show myself, which made my mother jump. Then she got stern again. "Karma, I told you to go to sleep!"

"Sorry, Mom, but I was waiting on Daddy. I can't sleep unless he's here."

"Awwwww," she said, giving way to a smile. "That shows great love for your father."

"I love my father, yes. But also rule number 177: 'Never go to sleep unless your father is present in the house. The only exceptions are if he is on an out-of-town trip or deceased."

Pride written all over his face, my father winked. "Time for bed, Karma. I'll tuck you in."

On the way to bed I could sense some tension in him. Even though he acted as if nothing was wrong, I could feel something wasn't right. While I was attempting to sleep, I noticed that my father was watching me. I didn't know exactly why. Still, my heart was content because all my family was in our secure home. I quickly fell asleep.

What I wouldn't find out until much later was what my parents talked about after my father came down to tell my mother what was going on with him and Steven. "Sincere, please tell me what happened. You seemed so worried than I've ever seen you since I met you."

Sincere looked at Eva and a tear began to fall from his eye. "For the past three years I've been getting to know Pastor Carson—to kill him. And now I truly don't think I can do it. He is a pure, innocent pastor. I couldn't find any type of bad bone in his body. Nothing but a few speeding tickets. Eva, I can't do this! I can't!" Sincere began to break down crying, which put fear in Eva's heart.

She never seen him cry or speak of any distrust about Steven's missions. For her to see both at the same time, this had to be a serious situation. Speechless and nervous, she held Sincere, like everything was going to be OK. To both of them, it seemed like they stood there forever, holding each other in silence. Finally Eva asked, "What do we do now?" My mother didn't care what the situation was or how deep it was. She was going to be with her husband till death do them part.

"We are going to take a family vacation."

"For good?"

"No, for two weeks," Sincere answered. "The kids' spring break is coming up and that's the perfect time to go. We'll act as if you had planned the vacation to surprise me. That will give me two weeks to find out why Steven wants Carson dead. I need you to go to work and brag about how you're planning to surprise me and the family with a two-week trip to the Dominican Republic. Tell them you picked that place because it's where I was born and you feel it would be good for me to show the kids where their bloodline started. And be sure to mention it to all the church members you work with."

That changed Eva from sad to confident. "No problem! I'll start on it in a couple days so it won't seem like this came up right after ya'll had your meeting."

Sincere gave her his biggest smile. "That's my girl!" After that, they made sweet love and Sincere held Eva while she slept. He couldn't sleep at all that night. All he could think about was that if he betrayed Steven how it would affect his family—a legend that had been going on long before his birth. For someone who had once been so certain about everything, he now found his thoughts confused. Was Pastor Carson's life that important that he should betray his legacy? Sincere needed answers, quick, and possibly a sign. In mid-thought, he got off the bed, fell to his knees and began to pray. He asked God for a sign.

After his prayer, Sincere could finally fall asleep. He dreamed one of the most innocent and purest dreams he could ever dream. He was an innocent boy in a field of crime. Terrible things were happening all around him, yet he heard only silence. All he could see was the crimes, and the expressions on the faces of the people who were hurting others, and of the people being hurt. He saw anger and he saw sadness. In his dream, he began to shoot the people who were hurting the others. He walked down a pathway of clouds, killing the criminals, he started to notice something that frightened him. The people he was saving, he realized, were the criminals and they were hurting other people. He was saving them and killing them at the same time. Then he saw a girl up ahead. When he reached her he recognized his daughter—me, Karma—who was being hurt. He sees I was being hurt by Steven. In his dream, Sincere was still a boy; he went to my defense, fighting with Steven and eventually killing him. Sincere looked back to see me saying, "Thank you," as I disappeared into the clouds. "Karma! Karma!" Sincere began to search for me. "Karma! Karma! Where are you? Please don't leave me!" Sincere began to cry, just like the child he was in the dream. Then suddenly a light began to emerge and he saw me appear with a knife, attempting to stab my mother. "Karma! Noooooo! Stop!" But I didn't stop. I stabbed Eva in the chest. Instantly, she started to bleed. In tears, Sincere ran to Eva. "Karma! Why would you do that? Why would you kill your mother?" Holding his wife, he pleads to God not to take her. Eva gasped for her last breath then she was dead. Breathing heavily, he ran to me, grabbed my shirt and asked once again, "Karma! Why would you kill your mothers? Why?" Without showing any emotion or sympathy, I simply replied, "Because you made me this way." Suddenly I transformed into Steven and Sincere woke up in a cold sweat.

Now he knew he'd dreamed the right dream. After his dream, Sincere knew he had to find out the real reason Steven wanted Carson dead. He realized he didn't just want to know, he had to. He had to know for my sake, and for the sake of our entire family's history.

Of course, I didn't know any of this when I woke up the next morning. As soon as I opened my eyes, I could smell the delicious aromas of a great breakfast being prepared for me and my sisters. I jumped up to get ready for the morning's training so I could be back in time for breakfast. After my run went to the pool for my timed swim. My Monday training included pushups, pull-ups, jumping jacks and sit-ups, then thirty minutes of non-stop hits and kicks to the boxing bag. After a quick shower I came down to eat with my family. Even though I felt a little tension with my father, something was different today. He seemed more confident and happier, which made me feel confident that everything was OK. As I began to eat my breakfast, I read my next killing assignment as if it was the newspaper. Now that I was thirteen, I couldn't discuss my killings with my father. He knew every mission I was assigned to, but

I was trained to act as if he didn't. I was not to discuss it or ask for any advice. The purpose was to make me stronger, point blank.

After breakfast, before leaving the house, my mother stopped me at the door to inform me we were going to surprise my father with a family trip to the Dominican Republic! I was toooo excited. I knew our family's roots were there but I had never been. I didn't want to be the reason we wouldn't leave on time so I decided to complete my mission before we left.

Anyway, the mission was simple. I didn't even have to get to know the person I was killing. All I had to do was creep through the bushes and shoot him point blank. He was kind of important, the mayor of a big city in South Carolina. I didn't find out much about him, because that wasn't my mission. I already knew he was a dirty mayor, who had taken money to do favors instead of serving all the people. He'd helped corrupt cops get away with murdering drug dealers and stealing their cash, including young, street-level dealers who might have been able to go straight if they'd gotten a chance. The mayor didn't care about any of this; he was just obsessed with money.

Most of the time I'm able to allow my victims to ask for forgiveness, but there are other times where all I could do was kill them. The older I got, the more I realized it's not my job to try to save them all. Just try to save as many as possible. I haven't met target who I felt should live. All of them were mean, cold-hearted people. Still, I didn't judge, because I was a cold-hearted person myself. I killed and I had no remorse for the killings I've done. So I was going to kill the mayor as soon as possible. I figured a nice gunshot to the head and one to the chest would do. I had two weeks to do it but decided I could watch his daily routine for four days then kill him on the fifth day.

So many thoughts were going through my head after Mom told me about the surprise for Daddy. I wanted to learn about the Dominican Republic so I would know my way around before I got there. I also wanted to know as much as I could about my family history. I'd begun to notice that I didn't know any-thing about my ancestors. So after school and my time with Christian, I went home and questioned my father. Just like in school, I was always very obser-vant and curious. I wasn't ever nervous about asking my father about anything, no matter how controversial the question was.

I loved the fact that I'd been trained to worship God and kill for him. It was my destiny to be others' karma. I was a born killer and I loved it.

"Kids, I'm home," Daddy yelled from the front door, his way of being sure to receive special warm hugs from his daughters.

"Hey, Daddy!" Of course all of us were excited to see him. It always felt great to see him. No matter what might be on his mind that bothered him, he never showed it. He always smiled. As soon as my father came home I wanted to ask him about our ancestors, but first I allowed my sisters to get their time in. I knew we were going to have to train later so I figured I would ask him then. First it was Kayren's turn. My oldest sister talked with him about getting accepted to Florida State on a full scholarship for criminal justice. She had already been in school for four years but now she was going back. I was proud of my sister, of course, but she was still with that no-good boyfriend, following the colleges he went to. She could have gone to Harvard but she decided to stick with that punk. My father didn't interfere; he said she has to experience life herself.

Next, he listened as Santana talked about her strong belief in God and how she was studying to become a minister.

Tennessee told him about being captain of the volleyball team and her above-the-class average.

He even heard about Sariah and Kariah trying out for the swim team. My father was always excited to hear about his daughters' accomplishments.

Finally, everyone else was finished and it was me-and-Daddy time. "OK, Karma! Ready for some training? You know the drill. Hundred sit-ups, pull-ups, pushups. After that, your run and your swim. We only got three hours before dinner, so let's go." I was so eager to get started I almost forgot that I had a question to ask him. "Daddy, I was wondering. If we've been killing for so long and it's always been passed down from generation to generation, then why don't I have a grandfather?"

He thought about it for a minute, but when he answered, it sounded like he'd been waiting for this question for a long time. "Well, Karma, that's our curse. We kill for God but sometimes in the process we get killed. That's why I wanted to make sure I had a big family. I wanted to break the chain. You see, my grandfather only had my father, who only had me. But I broke the chain when I had seven girls. I lied to your mother when I told her my mother was a killer. I didn't want her to get nervous if we only had girls, which is what happened. But I'm here to tell you that you are our very first female to ever kill for God. I feel there's a special reason for that."

For years I'd thought I was the family's second or maybe the third female to become a killer for God. But now, to find out I was the first of my kind. I began to put my skills on a pedestal. Maybe I was starting to get a little above myself. "So Daddy, are you saying I'm the only female that ever killed in our family history ever?"

"Yes, ever!"

"Daddy, you said that Granddaddy and Great-Granddaddy were the best killers in the world and that they were untouchable like we are. How were they killed? And were their ancestors killed?"

For a second it seemed like my father was in deep thought before he replied. "We all have our day when God calls upon us to come home."

Even though I believed my father, I still had so many questions to ask him. Still, I held them back and began my training. I must admit that after that conversation, I trained ten times as hard. Just like my father, I wanted to break the chain and live. I wanted my future kids to live and have the life that I never had. Now don't get me wrong. I love my life and killing for God, but deep inside, if I could change my family history I would. My goal was to protect my father, making sure we broke the family chain so we all could live!

After the day's training was finished, I wanted to prepare for my next mission so I could get it over with before our family trip. That mission was to kill another kid my age who had been corrupted. Her name was Shelly. As a child, she'd been mentally abused by her father. He would call her all types of names and also hit her from time to time for no reason. Her father lived a double life. He was a successful teacher in the day but a heavy drinker and a wife-and-daughter abuser at night. Shelly allowed his abuse until she was thirteen. Then she killed her father in cold blood, in a clever way that kept the law from even suspecting her. Now that was not the problem at all for me or for Christian. He was now assigning some of my missions, taking over part of his father's duties.

The problem for us was that Shelly now thought she should do the same thing to any father she ever heard yelling or even speaking loudly to his children. A few months after she'd killed her father, she was in the street and heard a stranger speaking strictly to his son about his behavior. The next day the father was dead, in what the police thought was an accident. Shelly had automatically assumed the child was being abused and took it upon herself to give the child justice. Then she did it a second time, after she saw a man spank his little girl in the supermarket.

The problem was that the fathers she was killing were good men. They weren't child abusers nor were their child-rearing ways bad. They just reinforced their children.

Christian had read in the paper about these men's mysterious deaths so he sent me to handle it. That's how I met Shelly. It's weird, because they say in life that mothers can tell who is a mother, gay people can tell who is gay or not and I guess a killer knows another killer when we see one. As soon as I saw Shelly, I knew she was a killer. I didn't know if she was the one I was looking for at the time but I knew she was one. It was a feeling I got as soon as I saw her. Such a weird feeling!

Anyways, I began to get to know her just like I did to the others I've targeted in other missions. To everybody who knew her, Shelly was a nice girl. She went to church, studied the Bible every day, she had good grades in school, she even helped with the elderly after school. The only problem was that her mind had been abused so badly that she was mentally messed up. Internally, I blamed her father for that, but he was already dead. I had to kill her unless I could get a feeling that she would change. For a week I studied her. I knew her every step and what time she did her daily routines.

I even witnessed one of her murders. She didn't know I was watching when I saw her kill a man in cold blood. That was hard for me, but her crime caught me off guard. Seeing this, I realized everything she did was at the spur of the moment. She was not the kind of person who would do any planning at all. The day I was watching her, she saw a father yell at his child. And she killed him that same day. Point blank. Little did she know the man was a father of three kids; he never beat them, but on that particular day he had just lost his job and was extra frustrated with one of his children. His anger was natural. As a matter of fact, before Shelly caught up with him, he felt so guilty he apologized to the child with tears in his eyes. The sad part is that Shelly was so focused taking revenge on him that she didn't see the sincerity in his heart.

Seeing this convinced me. She had to go! Something I'd learned about her gave me my chance. I'd let her known that I was interested in Bible study, just like she was. But I pretended I had a hard time concentrating at home and asked if we could meet somewhere quiet and talk about our lessons.

"I got the perfect place!" Shelly told me. "My church has a back door they don't lock, so people can go in and pray if they want. We could go there and study in one of the Sunday-school rooms." That was perfect. We made a date to meet there on a school night.

As soon as we got started, I offered her a bottle of water. She didn't know I'd spiked it with a potion that I'd made. It knocks out someone her age and size for an hour.

When she awoke she found herself in chains. Shelly screamed, "Why am I chained up? Who are you?" I was covered in all black and didn't reveal my face because I still felt she had a chance to live. Calmly, I replied, "I can't tell you my name or who I am. What I will tell you is that you might die tonight."

I could tell she was terrified. She was facing exactly what she'd done to those innocent men. "What do you mean, I might die tonight? You're not God. You're just a kid like I am." She couldn't see me, but she could hear my voice. I guess that gave me away.

"Maybe I'm a kid; maybe I'm not. But the point is, you've been killing other kids' fathers around town, with no remorse. I can't have that! I can't allow you to keep killing the good."

"What you mean? Kill the good? Those men yelled and abused their kids!"

"How do you truly know that? You don't even investigate these men. You don't give them a chance. Little do you know, these men aren't child abusers. They are good men who sometimes speak strictly to their children. That's all. They're not like your father. They don't call their kids bitches, hoes or sluts. They don't hit on their wives or their kids. I've done research; the men you killed didn't have any violent records. Not like your father."

I could see this was confusing Shelly. She said, "I killed these men because I wished someone would have killed my father for me and my mother. I wish someone would have stood up for me like you're standing up for these fathers. Where were you then, huh?"

"Where was I? I was training to kill people like you. But tonight you have a choice. You can stop killing and have a normal life. Right here, right now. You're in church; it's the perfect place to ask forgiveness. Let go and let God. Or you can die tonight."

I guess I must have offended Shelly because now she got angry. "I won't never stop!" She started laughing. "You don't get it, do you?"

"No, Shelly, I don't! Please explain."

By this time tears was running down her face. I could see the anger she'd been holding back. "My father fucked me more then he beat me. He was a terrible man. I even aborted his child. And you got the nerve to say I don't deserve justice. You're saying that if I see a bad man that he don't deserve to die?"

"I'm not saying that. What I'm saying is that the men you're killing are good men who don't deserve to die."

"What the fuck ever! You don't know! And you're not going to kill me. Because if you wanted to, you would have already."

I guess she didn't know who she was dealing with, huh? Bang! Straight shot to the side of her head. Shelly died instantly. As the blood began to leak from her head I removed the chains she was tied up with, and carefully put the pistol in her hand. As a final touch, I opened her Bible to the place where Judas commits suicide, and laid her head on the page. That should give the police all the explanation they needed.

May her soul rest in peace. Ashes to ashes, dust to dust!

Chapter 9

Vacation!

After my mission, I was excited about surprising my father and telling him about our family vacation. But my mother made me wait till the day of to tell him. So since I had two days until the trip, I decided to surprise him with my school grades.

"Report card time, girls!" My father was always eager to see our progress in our classes. We showed him our grades in the order we were born. First Kayren, then Santana, Tennessee, Sariah, Kariah, Destiny and last, but not least, me. Karma. I was so excited to show my father my grades; I rushed to his office as soon as my name was called. "Have a seat, my seventh daughter." It was time to wait quietly for his lecture before he looked at my grades. "Karma, you already know that I view all your grades separately so there won't be any competition in learning. I want you all to feel special in every way. I want you to succeed in life without discouragement about each other's accomplishments. So first, I want you to tell me your goals in school. Then I want you to show me your grades."

This was the moment I'd been waiting for. "Daddy, I want to play basketball for my high school." He didn't react right away, but just looked at me to let me know he was listening. So I went on. "I know I'm only thirteen and I'm in the ninth grade because of getting skipped up a grade a time or two, but I feel I can play with the bigger girls. And even start!"

I had been afraid my father wouldn't allow it because I already have such a busy schedule. But with a huge smile on his face, he replied, "Karma, that is a great idea. I know you can do it. I regret not living my own childhood to the fullest because I had so much work with Steven, but I'm so proud that you're living your child hood like you promised you would!"

"Yes, Daddy, I am. I will be trying out for the team in three weeks. I'm so excited! I've planned it where it won't affect my missions for God. I've been doing a lot of research about the basketball team's schedules, all the games and practices."

"Great job, Karma. I am so proud of you. At the age of thirteen, you're already on top of your generation. Steven said you're the best we ever had: ten kills and no mistakes! Even your father had a mistake at my eighth."

"Thank you, Daddy." With the hard part over so easily, now I was ready for the easy part. "And now, here are my grades."

As he took my report card, his eyes became very big. He began to smile extra hard. "Wow. Thirteen, two grades ahead of your class, and also top of your class with straight A's! Amazing, Karma. Amazing! A father couldn't be prouder!"

I was mighty proud, too, not just of what I'd done, but of what he thought of me. "Thank you, Daddy."

"Your training is also becoming perfect," he said. "You are a lethal boxer, you finish you miles in swimming, you run twice as fast as I expect. Christian says you're doing great, reading the Bible and learning just as well as he expects, too, which is a great feeling in my heart." I thanked him for all the compliments. "Anything you want to ask me Karma?"

I shook my head. "No, Daddy."

"OK, Karma. Enjoy the rest of your day and have fun with Christian. I heard today is fun day, so enjoy! Oh, one more thing. Since you were a little child, you never cried. The doctor says nothing is wrong with you. So now I'm asking you: have you ever wanted to cry but couldn't?"

"No, Daddy, actually I've never wanted to cry. I can't miss something I never experienced, so it doesn't bother me at all."

"OK. Great. Just checking on my seventh."

We ended our conversation with smiles and hugs and I went to my room to prepare for my fun day with Christian.

This is something we do twice a year, after report cards. I enjoy fun day with Christian because we finally get to see each other's fun side. We get to go to Fun World and play games, go fishing and rock climbing and then decide together what our last fun event will be. Christian was on time, ready to go. Steven and my father take turns taking us out on fun day and this time it was Steven's turn.

When they came to pick me up, I got an idea to show Steven and Christian my mission skills. Before they knew I was even outside yet, I had picked the lock on the back of Steven's SUV and sneaked into the back seat.

Steven started to get impatient, wondering where I was. He was about to beep his horn again when I whispered, "I'm here."

Steven turned around, shock on his face, then broke into a grin. "Karma, you scared me! Wow! How you do that?"

"I wanted you to see how my skills are improving every day. Hey, Christian."

"Hey Karma." I could tell he was impressed, too.

Steven said, "I see you're definitely improving. I'm impressed. But now, our next step is Fun World. Are ya'll ready?"

As soon as we got there I was ready for laser tag. After an hour of that, we rode go-carts for an hour, then rode all the rides. Even so, he had a blast. Next we went to the pier to calm down, fished for two hours, then we went back to the rock climbing wall for two more hours. Finally, it was time to agree on how we wanted to finish our day. Christian and I looked at each other and yelled, "Fun World!"

Steven was more than happy to go around a second time, and so we rode all the rides again. It was great!

I always loved fun day. After so much training, it helped me relax. I'm always so serious with my missions and staying focused that I don't usually get time out to have fun. When Steven dropped me off home, I told him about the secret trip my mother was planning for my father and how excited I was to go. I made him promise he wouldn't spoil the surprise by telling my father. Steven agreed and told me to have a safe and lovely trip.

Before I went to bed that night, I began to plan. I was going to take three bags. Since we would be on an airplane, I knew I couldn't take my guns or knives, but I could take my Bible and other training supplies. While my sisters were excited about the Jacuzzi, teen parties and great weather, I was looking forward to a twenty-mile run on the tropical beaches, swimming in the Caribbean and practicing kick-boxing with my father. I packed my boxing gloves, swimsuit and running shoes while my sisters were packing their hang-out outfits, bikinis and sunglasses.

I didn't mind anymore that I was different from my sisters, nor did I envy them for living normal lives. Actually, I was happy that I was their protector.

Finally, the day came to tell Daddy about the trip. After my mother gave us the go-ahead, my sisters and I ran up the stairs and shouted, "Daddy! Surprise! We're going on a trip!" We'd done it. We really had surprised him.

"Are y'all joking with me?"

Destiny grinned and replied, "No, Daddy, we're not joking. We're really going on a trip to see the beautiful water!"

I said, "Yep! Pack up!"

He began getting ready;

My mother came in to give him a hug and a smile. "Plane leaves in three hours. The kids are so excited!"

Everything was going perfectly. Until I saw Kale coming through the front door with his luggage. He greeted everyone with a hug and smiles but all I could do was mean-mug him. I wouldn't shake his hand or give him a hug. In my eyes, he was a dead man. I was just waiting on him to screw up. Since our little fight he'd been good but I knew he was going to slip up one day. And on that day, I will be there to catch his ass and kill him.

Soon after Kale came in the house, Kayla showed up with her luggage.

"Hey, Kayla! You coming too?" I was soooooo happy to see her, I didn't care too much that Kale was there. I was more excited about Kayla and me having fun and making Kale's life miserable. She greeted me with huge hugs and smiles. It had been a while since I'd seen her because of how much time I'd spent on my missions and all the extra training. I used to be that we'd have plenty of time to spend together in school, when I was skipped up two grades it was impossible for us to hang out. Still, we talked on the phone and texted every day and night. She was more than just my best friend; she became my seventh sister.

After Kayla and I put our luggage in the car, we went to my room to chill until it was time to go "Karma," she said, "I'm guessing you didn't know Kale was coming?"

"No. I didn't know that son of a bitch was going to be here."

Kayla smiled. "I'm also guessing that you're planning to mess him up while we're on the trip."

I gave her our friendship hand shake and said, "You already know!" We began laughing.

Pretty soon, Mom yelled, "Karma! Kayla! Time to go!"

I gave Kayla a confidential wink. "Let's get it. Last one down got to sneak-trip Kale before we get on the airplane." Without taking the time to agree, Kayla began to run, trying to beat me to the truck. I walked quietly, without any rush at all. When I got to the truck, Kayla smiled and said, "You wanted to lose.

I laughed. "You know it!"

As soon as we got to the airport, I was ready to start making Kale's trip with us as miserable as I could.

Kale, of course, was trying to be the saint. He offered to carry Mom's and Kayren's bags. He didn't know I was carrying something special, too: a little invention of mine I call silk oil. As we got into the terminal, I splashed some of it in Kale's path. As soon as his foot hit the oil, his ass hit the floor and the bags flew everywhere. People in the airport began laughing, including Kayla and me. The fall was even funnier than I'd imagined. Kale looked up to see the two of us bugging our asses off at him. He was sooooo embarrassed and pissed but couldn't show his anger because of my father being there.

As soon as my father saw Kale on the floor and me laughing my ass off, he knew his fall wasn't an accident. Daddy pulled me to the side and said, "Karma, I know you don't like Kale. I also know you were responsible for his fall. I know you and Kayla want to have fun on this trip so all I ask is, don't kill him. Promise!"

"Yes, Daddy, I promise!"

My father didn't like Kale that much, either, but he didn't want to lose Kayren. He knew that if he was to show his dislike for Kale, it was possible that it could distance his relationship with his daughter. So he played it cool.

Me, on the other hand? I was going to make Kale's trip miserable whether Kayren liked it or not. Plus I didn't plan for her to know what Kayla and I would be doing. On the airplane, I was mostly asleep. I'd been so excited about going on the trip that I hadn't slept a lot the night before. Also, the missions I'd just completed had taken a lot of energy.

After the killings I've done, you would have thought I wouldn't be able to sleep at all, but I slept just like a baby.

Finally, after a long but nice plane ride, we were here. The Dominican Republic looked more beautiful than I'd expected. The water was blue like the morning sky after a storm has passed. The weather was perfect, like a newborn to its parents. I couldn't believe the scenery was so perfect. I couldn't wait to train here. The first day was full of fun and play. The family took a boat to a smaller island, several miles out to sea. I had to beg my father to allow me to swim there while the family rode the boat, which was paddled by the resort's staff. I must admit my father was nervous. My mother was scared to death. To ensure that I was safe, my father brought binoculars so he could keep an eye on me. To my family's amazement, I reached our destination before the rest of them did.

Daddy was so proud, but I could tell he was distracted, focused on something else. I couldn't read him and his thoughts but I could tell something was wrong. While my sisters and I enjoyed the little island we were visiting, my father left to go off by himself. I figured maybe he had a mission, but then again, this trip had been a surprise. He couldn't have had time to plan a mission here. But even though I was having a weird feeling about my father's behavior, I took it as just me being paranoid. I brushed the feeling off. So while my father was away, I was busy playing with my family. And making Kale have a terrible trip.

I noticed there was a church on the island and it looked like my father was heading that way. I wondered why, but still I brushed it off and kept playing.

What I didn't know was that my father really was on a mission. When he went off to walk to that church, even though his family was on vacation, it was because he was determined to find out answers. He hadn't just randomly chosen to bring us out to this island; he was here for a reason. He'd known about our surprise trip all along, because he had planned it.

And here, in the little church on this little island, was the pastor he'd been assigned to kill. Sincere knew that Pastor Carson might be able to help him understand the reason Steven wanted him dead. It was a huge risk for Sincere to confide in Pastor Carson. He really didn't know how to approach him. Finally, he came up with a plan to confess his sins as if he was an average person. But first he had to come up with a disguise and get a weapon. He was determined that if he couldn't get any answers, he would kill the pastor.

Sincere was more anxious about this mission than any he'd ever done. He didn't want to go against Steven's wishes but he also didn't want to kill an innocent man. Sincere had never thought this day would come; but he had to be a man.

He dressed in old clothes and put on a fake beard as if he was a poor, elderly man. The church was wide open; two security guards watched the front doors, but they didn't question him. He went directly into the confessional. "Forgive me, Father, for I have sinned."

The pastor answered, "We all sin, my son, so please confess without any doubts about being judged."

"Father, I am a killer. I kill people who commit horrible sins. I've been killing ever since I was a child. My job is to kill for a pastor who talks to God; God tells him who needs to meet death. I'm not proud of my actions nor do I regret them but now I've been requested to kill a man I feel is innocent."

For a minute the confessional was quiet. Then the pastor spoke, calmly and confidently. "Hello, Sincere."

Amazed, Sincere said, "How do you know my name?"

"I've always known you. I always knew there would be a day I would be approached by you and that it could possibly be my day of death; or my new life. You see, twenty-three years ago, your father, Jeremiah, was in the same seat you were in. He also was sent to kill me."

Through tears of disbelief and anger, Sincere replied, "Wait! If my father was ordered to kill you twenty-three years ago, you would be dead! No questions asked! And it was twenty-three years ago that my father was murdered. So you have some fucking explaining to do." Sincere began to reach for his gun; in his mind, it seemed the pastor was trying to confess that he had killed Sincere's father.

"Sincere, please calm down. I was the reason your father was murdered. But it wasn't me or my people who killed him."

Still in tears, Sincere replied, "Explain! Now!"

"Son, please forgive me, because I should have protected him from Steven's father Lloyd. He's the one who killed your father."

"Liar!"

"No, son, I wouldn't lie to you. And please brace yourself, because what I'm about to tell you is very heart breaking. The whole life you been living has been a lie. Lloyd, Steven, all of that family are liars. You are not killing for God. You are killing for their benefit. You see, back when this all first started, my grandfather was the founder of what we call "God's wishes." He was the one who was tested by God. And yes, your ancestors were also tested by God. But not the way ya'll have been taught. You see, my great-great-great-grandfather's name was Caesar. I know you know the story about Caesar and how God talked to him. What you don't know is that Caesar had a best friend named Dathon. Once God told Caesar his destiny, he told his best friend Dathon about it. Dathon became jealous and began to curse God; he felt he should have been the chosen one. He couldn't understand what was so good about Caesar."

Sincere was so surprised by this that he couldn't say anything.

The pastor continued his story. "Dathon became so angry that he killed Caesar, then acted as if he was Caesar himself. Then he met with Karman. He knew the whole story so well that he convinced Karman he was the one chosen to speak for God. Since Karman had already committed sin, he was not able to hear the truth from God. Karman did hear words in his head, telling him not to trust this new Caesar, but he thought those words were the talk of the devil. That's because before God had asked Karman to commit a sin, he had also told him that afterwards he would not speak to him again. God had told Karman that the devil would have power to speak in his mind, and warned him not to listen to the devil's words. So Karman didn't. That's why Dathon was able to continue this lie for so long, through so many generations. Since his time, all of his future children and grandchildren have known this truth. They all chose to continue the lie and have ya'll kill innocent people."

The more he heard, the more it seemed to make sense to Sincere. The more his own uneasy feelings were now starting to make sense.

"Ya'll kill people for money," the pastor went on, "not the sins they commit. Have you noticed that the people you kill usually have money? Lots of cash? That's because Steven's family has been getting you and your ancestors to kill for their profit. That was not God's Plan. God believes in forgiveness. He don't want ya'll murdering people."

Now Sincere began to cry. He cried harder than he'd ever cried before. His thoughts and emotions were so confused; so many questions were going through his mind. How did Pastor Carson know these things about his family? Was he telling the truth or was this a trick? But even though Sincere was wanting so many answers, all he could do was cry. The noise must have gotten the security guards' attention. One of them came to the pastor's side of the confessional and knocked on the door.

Sincere reached for his gun.

The pastor answered the knock, "Yes, Son?"

"Sorry to interrupt, Pastor, but I was checking on you to see if you were OK. This has been your longest session ever, and then I heard something . . ."

Without any hesitation, Pastor Carson replied: "Everything is completely fine, and it might take longer. So ya'll, with my permission, can lock up the church and go have lunch."

"Are you sure?"

"Yes, I'm sure."

Sincere began to wipe his tears and finally was able to speak. "You felt confident enough to leave your life in my hands even though you know I'm here to kill you?"

"Son, you might think you're here to kill me but in reality you're here to find out the truth. For years, your father and his father and so on have all come here and found out the truth. Its destiny. The sad part is that after your ancestors found out the truth, each of you has been killed. You've been unable to pass on that truth; you've been unable to stop the sinful tradition. Before your father left this church, I warned and pleaded with him to stay. He wouldn't. He felt he had to confront and or kill the ones who'd created this, which is Steven's family."

Sincere stood up. He was ready to leave the confessional.

"Before you do anything," the pastor told him, "I must let you see my face." He opened the door on his side of the confessional and stepped out, where the two men greeted each other with a loving hug.

"I believe you," Sincere said, "but I still have doubts. Steven is someone I've trusted with my life. Since birth! I can't just turn my back on him."

"I have proof that I'm telling the truth." Pastor Carson pulled out a Bible and turned the pages until he came to a bundle of letters. The letters, he said, were from Sincere's father, grandfather and all his great-grandfathers. All the letters spoke of how they had been sent to kill Pastor Carson's ancestors. They revealed how all of them had doubts, and even stated the day that each one had decided not to kill the pastor. Every letter was dated and signed.

Sincere recognized his father's handwriting and signature. Once again, he began to cry. Sincere saw that his great-grand father, grandfather and father had each been killed three days after they'd written their letters. It all started to come in place in his mind. Sincere realized his ancestors had all been killed by Steven's ancestors.

"Pastor Carson, I have to go. Now I know the truth. I have to confront him."

"Please, Sincere. Don't! I beg you not to leave. Please, stay here. Start a new life and live!"

Sincere began to shake his head. "I can't do that. My life, my family's life is in Miami. I can't just ask them to give that up!"

"They love you, Sincere. And they would give all that up for you!"

Sincere pulled himself up straight and looked Pastor Carson in the eye. "I have an idea for how I can go kill Lloyd and Steven, and that will end it all. Christian and Karma will have a chance to live normal lives. But if I stay here, I will be running."

A tear began to fall from Pastor Carson's eye. "Please. Don't Leave! You may not come back!"

"I tell you what. I will write the same letter as my father did. I want you to keep it in your collection. I won't be killed; but if somehow I am, then I promise you: Karma will end the tradition. She is the smartest of our kind. I promise, she will end it. But please trust that I will end it as well. You will also be going back to Miami," he told the pastor, "and you shouldn't want to live your life in fear. Neither should I."

The pastor took a deep breath and replied, "Well, if there's no convincing you to stay, then I must let you leave and continue your journey. Goodbye, Sincere."

He and Sincere exchanged a last strong hug. "See you later, Pastor Carson!"

After Sincere departed, Carson dropped on his knees with tears on his eyes. He whispered a little prayer, asking God to watch over Sincere.

Sincere quickly returned to the side of the island where he'd left us, to find Kale trying to scream through a gag, tied up and hanging from the tree with a fire under him. Kayla and I were, of course, laughing and cooking marshmallows on the fire.

"Karma!" he shouted as sternly as he could. I could tell he was trying not to laugh. "What are you doing to Kale?"

"Hey, Daddy. Mom and the girls went for a swim by the waterfall and we decided to play a game with Kale, Mom wanted me to make a fire so we could make s'mores. Kale wanted to play. Ask him!"

Sincere began to sigh. "Karma, it's kinda hard to ask him a question when his mouth is taped up. Let him down. Now!"

"But Daddy—"

"No buts, Karma. Let him down now."

I could tell by my father's voice that he was serious now, so I did let him down. Just not very gently. Of course, he fell face down in the sand.

"Kayla, please untie Kale. I have to speak to my daughter." Daddy signaled that I should come with him and we began to walk down the beach. I knew for a fact that he was going to make a speech but I wondered why. He already knew I was going to mess with Kale. But whatever he had to say, he is my father so if he was about to tell me to leave the boy alone, then I would.

"Karma, you know I love you." I couldn't tell from that whether this talk would be a good one or bad.

"Yes, Daddy, I know."

"Well, it's time for you to grow up. You can't keep holding grudges, Karma. Life is filled with so much more joy than making others' lives miserable."

"You're right, Daddy, but I just don't like Kale. I don't hold grudges with any of my sisters' other boyfriends. Just him!"

"Karma, your other sisters don't have any boyfriends." He had me there.

"Oh. Well. I just don't like Kale."

"OK. I can't make you like him; so just be nice. But now I wanna talk to you about something else."

I could tell my father wasn't in a good mood. He seemed very sad, like someone had died or even like a part of him was dying. I couldn't understand why he was feeling this way while we were on such a beautiful trip. I mean, it's not like I'd killed Kale or anything. I was just messing with him, putting a little fear in his ear. That's all.

"Karma, I want you to promise me something."

I nodded. "Yes, Daddy. Anything."

"Promise me that before you go on another mission—before you kill any-one—that you investigate the situation yourself. Make sure you're doing the right thing." I thought that was strange. I looked hard at my father, not understanding what he was telling me. "We already do that. That's why we have Steven and Christian! They talk to God! Remember?"

My father gave me a sad smile. "Yes, Karma, I know. But just remember my words. remember that I love you and that I would never put you in any harm. OK?"

I couldn't really understand where this conversation was coming from. I really couldn't understand why my father was so distracted. Even so, I agreed to remember what he'd told me. We turned around and walked back to meet the family.

The rest of the trip my father seemed very sad. He tried not to show it, but it was obvious something was wrong. My father asked my mother to have a romantic dinner with him our last night on the beach while the girls and I went to a party. I really didn't want to go but my father wouldn't let my sisters go if I wasn't there, too. So after a lot of begging from my sisters I decided to tag along. It was cool, 'cause I figured Kayla could help me have a good time. We chilled at the party till midnight but then came back to our rental for the night. My sisters and Kayla were dead tired from partying so they decided to go to sleep. I wanted to train.

As late as it was, I decided a short, twelve-mile run would be about right. When I got back, I thought I heard something. I went to look for my father and found him holding my mother. She was crying harder than I had ever seen her cry.

"Mom, what's wrong?"

My father came to my side. I could tell he had been crying, too. "Karma, I thought you were asleep with your sisters."

"No, I decided to run."

He nodded. He always approved of how I pushed myself physically. But then he offered his explanation. "Well, your mother just got a call that her best friends died. She's taking it very hard. So go get some sleep while I spend time with your mother and try to console her." My father reached down and gave me a big hug. "I love you, Karma."

It felt like he held me tighter, and longer, than he usually did. "I love you too, Daddy!"

Chapter 10

Truth or death

Ever since the vacation my father had been sad and depressed. He wasn't eating much and for a week he allowed me to train by myself. I didn't know what was wrong but I knew it was really bad. I'd never seen my father like that. At all. Ever. I even walked in on him once, and found him crying and pleading to God, asking for forgiveness. I wondered why my father would ask for forgiveness when we had been obeying God's every wishes all along. So I decided I had to ask him what was wrong.

"Hey, Daddy, am I disturbing you?"

He didn't seem to mind that I'd seen him so upset. "No, Karma. Do you have something you need to talk to me about?"

"Yes, I've noticed you haven't been yourself lately. And I know exactly why."

He was shocked. "Karma, the information that you know could possibly not be true. I don't know for sure yet. I was going to tell you, but I didn't want you to be upset and discouraged."

"Well, Daddy, I am. I can't believe y'all are going to do this. There's another way."

"Karma, there is no other way. If I find out he's been lying to me, I'll have to kill him."

Now I was puzzled. "Kill who?"

My father looked back at me, confusion on his face. "What are you talking about, Karma?"

"I'm talking about you and Mom getting a divorce."

My father released a sigh and his face brightened right up. With a smile, he said, "Karma, why would you think your mother and I are getting a divorce?"

"Y'all both been sad and depressed. I've never seen y'all like that."

"I assure you, your mother and I are not getting a divorce. I promise! I am still deeply in love with your mother. Just like I was when we first met."

After my father said that, I was even more confused. "So why are you so sad?"

"When the right time comes, trust me, I am going to tell you everything. But until I get all my information, I can't tell you. I have to wait until the time is right."

As soon as he got the words out his mouth, the phone started to ring. "Karma, get that for me."

"Hello . . . . Hey, Mr. Steven! Our vacation was great . . . . Yeah . . . . Uh-huh . . . . I swam over thirty miles in the most beautiful water I've ever seen . . . . . Yes, Daddy is here . . . OK . . . Daddy! Telephone!"

He took the phone and turned to his study. Before he shut the door, he told, me, "Karma, go train. I want fifteen laps in the pool, two hundred push-ups and pull-ups, eighty kicks and punches to the big bag. Finish with your usual run around town. Then after your warm-up, we'll get to training."

"OK, Daddy. I'm on it." I instantly went to start my warm-up.

~

My father went into his study and closed the door. In his pocket, his device was set to "Record."

"Hey, Steven. How are you?"

"I'm doing great, Sincere. How was your trip?"

"It was relaxing. The kids had a great time and that's what fulfilled my heart."

"That's good, Sincere. I'm glad you enjoyed yourself. You deserved a great vacation. I was just talking with my wife; Sheila wants to cook a big dinner and have me to invite you and Eva to come. I figure after dinner the wives can have girl talk and we can get to business. About Pastor Carson."

"That sounds like a great idea. What time? And do you want me to bring the kids?"

"Well, if you want. But I was thinking that Christian could stay over there with your girls and the four of us have an adult dinner together."

"That sounds good to me."

Once they'd lined up all the arrangements and hung up, Sincere allowed himself a huge sigh. He didn't want Steven to think anything was wrong so he'd have his guard up. But when Steven left, he forgot to turn off his recorder. Which is how I eventually knew about what happened next.

A few minutes later, Eva walked in to find Sincere on his knees, once again, in prayer. "Where's Karma?" he asked.

"She's out training."

"What about the other girls?"

"Kayren's at the movies with Kale; Sariah and Kariah are at the skating rink; Santana's in Bible school; Tennessee is in her Mechanics for Kids class. And Destiny is in her room, asleep."

"OK. Great." Sincere knew it was time to bring Eva in on what was going to happen. "Steven called. He wants us to have dinner with him and his wife Monday night. At nine—"

"Well, I see he's not expecting anything wrong, huh?"

"No he's not, but I'm going to take my gear. If he can't give me the right answers to my questions, then it will be time for him to die! If Pastor Carson is telling the complete truth then I must end this curse. I can't allow Karma to continue the tradition if it's a lie."

Eva kissed Sincere on the forehead. "I got your back the whole way!"

Sincere looked at Eva with a look of love at first sight and began kissing her neck and gently touching her as if it was their first time, they began to make love in the study room. Eva's and Sincere's love was so strong and passionate that only God could break them. Sincere would die twice for Eva and she would do the same for him. Even though he had a lot on his mind, it didn't affect him from putting his love into action in the study. For an hour and thirty minutes, neither one had any concerns about the day to come.

~

Until I came back and found the door locked. I knocked. "Daddy, I'm finished warming up. You ready to train?"

"Wait at the door for one second, Karma!"

I didn't quite understand what I was hearing through the door; now I know it must have been Sincere and Eva getting dressed. "OK, Karma come in," he said.

I found my mother and father smiling in each other's arms. "Yes! No divorce!"

Mom replied, "Divorce?"

Daddy smiled at her and said, "Don't worry about that. I'ma go train with Karma. We will be home for dinner."

My father and I began our normal training and technique moves. He focused on my ability to disappear in certain situations. My next mission was tomorrow and I had a big chance of getting caught if I didn't do everything right. Three hours into my workout, it was finally time to take a fifteen-minute break. Of course my father wanted to talk and figure out how my mind was with this mission.

"Karma, you need any more water?"

"No, Daddy. I'm fine."

"So how do you feel about the mission tomorrow?"

"I feel good. I'm just wondering . . . how can someone be so cruel to be planning to kill a nursing home full of people?"

"Well, like Steven said we don't know for sure if he plans to do it but he did confess: not just what he plans to do but that it's supposed to happen tomorrow. Now I know Christian has told you about the guy and you know how he looks. But I'm a little nervous because this is your first time having to kill someone in daylight and in public."

"Daddy, I know. But I am trained for this. I know what I have to do and what I need to do. To be honest, I've been waiting for a mission like this because I know I'm being tested. Daddy, I promise I will pass the test."

"I believe you and I trust you are ready. You are thirteen and maturing day by day but if anything happen to you I wouldn't know how to live. My heart would die a thousand times because I know I'm the reason you're a killer."

I could tell my father was getting teary-eyed while expressing his love for me. I never knew the feeling of crying; seeing my father drop tears as much as he did since we been back from our vacation made me never want to know the feeling. I'd rather never cry than to feel so much pain. I still didn't know why my father was so sad but I could tell he was in pain. "Daddy, don't worry. I will be OK. You've trained me since I was born to become the best. I would never let you down. Ever! We're here to kill for God and I respect and understand that."

My father took a deep sigh as if I had said something wrong. "You're right, Karma and I love you."

"Love you too, Daddy."

"Great. Now we have two more hours. So go get your knives and swords."

I love this part of training! It's one thing to kill someone evil with a gun but I get the best feeling when I use a knife. I don't know why; it just feels better. After training it was time for me do some yoga in the quiet room, take a shower and meet my family for dinner.

My mother had cooked an awesome meal. Fried chicken, potato salad, green beans, ham, corn and some lovely buttered dinner rolls. I tore that food up! After dinner I read the Bible for three hours and was in bed by nine o'clock. I slept a wonderful sleep and got up at 5:30 a.m. to prepare for my possible kill today. My mission was kinda weird because I had to follow the suspect and wait until he tried to kill. I already knew what to look for but I was adjusted to just killing someone. I wasn't used to waiting till they try to commit a horrible crime. Still, I did what was told.

I watched him for hours and hours. He didn't try anything. Just when I was about to think he was just talk and no harm, I saw him placing loaded weapons in his car. I already knew what that was about. I jumped on my scooter and followed him to his destination, the Miami Christian Nursing Home. I already knew its capacity was five hundred elderly people. While my suspect sat in his car preparing his weapons, I stealthily climbed to the roof where I waited for him to try to enter the front door. Finally, I saw he was ready, getting out of his car with a big bag over his shoulder. The bag, of course, was full of guns. As he rang the doorbell, I dropped a rope and began to slide silently down, with my knife ready. Even before a worker could get to the door and open it, my suspect was falling to the floor, with a slit to the neck. When he fell, his bag came open and everything spilled out. He lay there, with his guns, dead. Inside the locked front door, the worker began screaming. "Call 911!"

But before the police had even been called, I was gone. An easy five-minute mission. No one saw me. And while they certainly questioned who had killed the man, seeing all his guns meant nobody wondered why. I felt so good. I had stopped a massacre. I went home and hugged my father, telling him how well I had done.

He was very proud of me. I felt that after the mission was over that he would go back to smiling and being happy again, but I was wrong. I could still see sadness in his eyes. Now I really began to wonder what was wrong with him. I'd seen him becoming depressed day by day. He still wasn't eating much and I even began to see him drinking more and more. His behavior was so weird. I didn't know what to do. I began to start wishing that we'd never gone on the trip because if we hadn't, then maybe he wouldn't have been so sad afterwards.

I wanted to make my father happy again. All my life, I always wanted to please him and make him happy. That's why I trained so and worked so hard to do well in school. So with him being sad, I began to be sad. The crazy part was that I didn't know what the hell we were sad about. I just could feel his pain.

After a week of sadness and still feeling my father's pain, I decided to call Steven and ask him if he knew what was wrong. When Steven picked up the phone, he greeted me with a wonderful but surprising hello.

"Pastor Steven, can I meet you somewhere and talk?" He seemed happy to agree, and we set a time after my Bible study with Christian. I was so anxious to talk to Steven. I knew he had all the answers and that he would be able to tell me why my father was so sad. Just as we'd planned, as soon as I was done with Christian I went to Steven to begin with all the questions that had been boggling my mind.

He greeted me warmly. "Karma, of the thirteen years I've known you, we never had a meeting like this. I must admit I was extremely surprised."

"I wouldn't have broken the rules if this wasn't extremely important," I explained. "You see, Daddy has been very sad since we took our trip. I don't know what's wrong with him. Is he OK?"

"Well, Karma, I haven't seen the sadness you've seen in your father the past month, but I will definitely find out what's going on. Did your father tell you about the dinner we're having for your parents tomorrow? Maybe that will cheer him up."

"You're right, Pastor Steven. That might cheer him up! Thank you. And keep this between us because I don't want Daddy knowing that I broke our rules by talking to you and not Christian."

Steven replied with a smile. "I was thinking the same thing. Have a great night, Karma."

I left Steven's house and began to run home as usual. Steven only lived a few miles away so I wasn't tired at all when I got home. I decided to work out some more. I loved to work out no matter how late or early it was. I was excited about my father's dinner with Steven tomorrow. I was ready to see him happy again.

The next day, though, my father was still looking a little sad but also very focused, which was weird. I mean, he was just going to a dinner! But because he'd been acting so weird ever since we got back, I didn't pay it much attention. I was in the quiet room kick-boxing when he stuck his head in the door and asked to speak to me before dinner.

After I'd cleaned up and sat down with him, he said, "I've been wanting to have this talk for a long time. I want you to know that I love you and will always love you. The life I birthed you in was the life I thought was your destiny. I would never put you in any danger or harm. You know that, right?"

"Yes, Daddy, I know."

"Well, also know that you are the family's protector and it's your duty to protect our family. Always protect your family! Never regret your past. And remember: you have a future." And then Daddy started to cry. He grabbed me close.

"Daddy, why are you so sad?"

"Karma, I'm sad now. But after my dinner with Steven, I'm sure I will be happy again."

It made me smile to see my father wiping away his tears. I already knew about the dinner and Daddy had just confirmed what Steven had told me yesterday. I was ready to get my happy, loving father back and this dinner was going to do it.

While my parents were preparing for dinner I was working out: lifting weights, calisthenics and swimming. I didn't even see them leave; just heard my father yell, "Karma, we're leaving."

"OK. Have fun!"

~

While driving to Steven's house, Sincere could feel his gut in his toes. He had a feeling it would be dangerous to carry his recorder with him, so he hid it in the car's trunk. But a miniature microphone in a button on his jacket was transmitting everything.

Eva looked at him and asked, "Sincere, are you OK?"

"Yes, baby, I'm OK. I'm just a li'l nervous, that's all."

"Everything's going to be OK."

"I know, baby. It's just this been on my mind for weeks and now it's finally time to confront him." Eva began to kiss Sincere on his ear so he could relax a little.

At Steven's house, they went straight to the dinner table. At first there was silence. Then Eva broke the ice. "So Steven, how is the new church coming along?"

"It's going great. We should be finished in two more weeks. Matter of fact, we should go look at it tonight, after dinner."

"That would be great," Eva replied. There was some tension at the dinner table, but still Steven acted like he couldn't tell anything at all was wrong with Sincere; it was as if he was ignoring his pain. After dinner, as he'd said, Steven insisted on Sincere and Eva going to see his new church.

Sincere agreed, but first, he said, he wanted to talk business with Steven.

Steven agreed, but he wanted to have that talk after visiting the church.

So they all went. As soon as they got to the church, Eva and Sincere were amazed. The new building was so beautiful. The inside of the sanctuary was long and high, with gold walls. The floor was covered with bright carpet and the walls were painted with angels, white and black, with wings so white you would have thought they were real.

Taking it all in, Sincere saw something he didn't understand. He asked, "What are the golden cages for?"

"They're for the white doves. This church is about to be the new beginning for us. Don't you see how wonderful this is? This is what we've been working hard on."

"Yes, Steven I see." Sincere continued to look around the church.

~

Back at home, meanwhile, the girls and I began to play a few games to pass the time away. Christian didn't come over; we heard that he was sick. But after a while, I began to get tired of playing games with my sisters. I decided to go to Steven's house. I wanted to be the first to see my father smile again.

It didn't take me long to run over there, but Steven's wife informed me that he and my parents were at the new church. I estimated that it would be another twenty minute run, so off I went. While running, I was getting more and more excited about seeing my father smile again—and also seeing the new church.

~

Sincere was admiring it, too. "Steven, I must admit the church is beautiful."

"We have worked extra hard on this and it's finally completed. God will be pleased. Now, Sincere: what did you have to talk to me about?"

"It's very important. But how 'bout Eva go and wait in the car while we have our conversation."

Steven waved his hand and shook his head. With a tone he must have meant to sound reassuring, he said, "No, she should stay here. I mean she does know everything and I'm sure she is a very good confidant. And I know you didn't hide anything from your wife. So it's best if she stay."

That didn't hit Sincere quite right. He wanted to question Steven's reason for wanting Eva to stay, but instead he got down to business. "Steven, when I went on my family vacation a few weeks ago, it wasn't for a family vacation. It was actually to find out answers."

Steven looked like he was a little surprised. "Answers to what?"

Sincere swallowed hard and got right down to it. "I couldn't figure out why you wanted me to kill a pastor so bad. What was so bad about him. I knew Pastor Carson would be on vacation at the same place so I needed to go to him for answers."

Steven looked very serious as he replied, "Why would you need to go ask questions about something we've been doing since birth? I ask you to kill; you kill. That's it. No questions! Understand?"

"Yes, I understand. That's how it's been forever." Sincere looked Steven in the eye. "But you wanted me to kill an innocent man. You had no reason to kill him. So now I ask: why did you want him dead?"

"I wanted him dead," Steven answered without hesitating, "because he was going to destroy what we have. Sincere, I refuse to let him take away our tradition! We have something that's more important than you, me, our families. We have to keep justice in the world. I talk to God; you kill for God. That's how it's been and that's how it always will be!"

"I understand that, Steven. But was your family really meant to be the ones who were supposed to kill for God? Or was the real Caesar the one? And your ancestor took his life to become him?"

Now Steven let his anger show. "You shut your fucking mouth, Sincere! I always knew you would be too weak for this mission! You just proved me right, But yes, yes, yes. We killed to be here. And yes, each of our generations has been lying to each of your generations. But it is what it is. We would have told y'all the truth . . . except that y'all were all weak! That's why we didn't tell y'all. Your hearts couldn't stand it. Your family might be strong at killing, but when it comes to this, y'all don't have the heart for it. Let's be honest!"

Sincere began to get red in the face. "I am strong!"

"Yes, Sincere, you are. But not strong at doing things that may feel wrong! You are sooooooo weak when it comes to that! Your whole family is!"

That was too much for Sincere. He leaped onto Steven and began choking him. "You have no right to say that about my family! We shed out blood for you and you have the nerve to say we're weak! Fuck you!"

"No, Sincere, fuck you!" Steven punched Sincere in the face and turned to run up the stairs to the top of the church tower.

Sincere pulled out his gun.

Eva screamed, "No, Sincere!"

From where he stood, Sincere squeezed off two shots, then moved, gun up and ready, to follow up the stairs behind Steven

Eva followed him, screaming, "Sincere! Stop! He's not worth it!"

Sincere's anger kept him going until he reached the top of the church tower, seven flights up, to find Steven on the roof, standing at the railing, his hands up.

"Sincere. This is how you're going to do me? This is how you're going to end all that we have created?"

Waving the gun at him, Sincere replied, "Yes! I refuse for Karma to become a lie like I have." Tears began to roll down his face.

Eva caught up with him, tears in her eyes, too. "Sincere, you don't have to kill Steven! We can just walk away."

Steven couldn't help some sarcasm: "Yes, Sincere! Walk away!"

Sincere was about to pull the trigger when a thought stopped him. He remembered that he didn't want to be a killer anymore. He also thought about what Eva had said: that Steven was not worth breaking his promise to God. Sincere shook his head and began to lower his gun.

Eva sighed with relief.

Steven smiled, showing all his teeth. "That's what I thought. Weak." He waited half a second, then yelled, "Christian! NOW!"

Christian came out of the darkness behind the stairway and pushed Eva over the railing.

Sincere screamed, "Noooooo!" and aimed his gun to shoot Christian. He didn't notice Steven running as fast as he could to push Sincere off the top of the tower.

~

That was the moment that I finally reached the church, finding my father's car parked in front. I smiled in relief that they were still there. I was about to go into the church when out of nowhere I heard a crash on the front of the car, then another crash on the back. The impacts were so strong that they jerked me back against the church door. But my training had served me well; even after that jolt, I hurried right back to the car—where I found my mother and my father, both dead.

At first, all I could do was stand there. I was speechless. Both my parents were lying in front of me, bloody, and dead. A strong pain began to come over my body from my toes to my head. In my head, I began to feel a sharp pain that I'd never felt before. Suddenly, tears began to fall from my eyes. I was so hurt. I'd never felt pain like that before in my life. I leaned over the crumpled car and hugged my father, trying to wake him up.

"Daddy, wake up, please wake up!" Then I turned to my mother. "Mom . . . Please!" The tears began to flow harder and harder. "Daddy! Mom!" For the first time in my life, I found myself crying. Then I realized I was covered in blood. My parents' blood. "Nooooooooo!" I couldn't stop the tears streaming down my cheek.

Then, suddenly, a hand touched my shoulder. It was Steven. "Karma, I tried to help your father. I tried to make him happy again. He was just too sad. I asked him to come here with me, but he insisted on climbing to the top of the tower. I could see what he was thinking, but I was too far away. Your mother tried to stop him and while he was resisting her, he accidently pushed her over the edge. Then he really went crazy. He was so distraught about what he'd done that he jumped after her."

I couldn't speak. I could barely hear what Steven was saying. All I could do was run. Without a word, I took off. I must have stopped for food and water, but all I can remember is running for days and through the nights. I ran until my feet became swollen and bloody. Even after that, I ran and ran. All I could think about was my mother and father lying on our car, covered in blood. Finally, all my training couldn't help me anymore. I was out of energy, but still I wouldn't quit. My body decided for me: I passed out.

Next thing I remembered was lying in the hospital with Steven, Christian and my sisters around my bed. With a sad smile, Steven said, "Karma, I'm so glad you are OK! We were all worried about you. You've been here, unconscious, for four days now."

"Where's my mother and father?"

My sisters began to cry. Kayren spoke up. "They're gone to a better place, Karma."

And once again, tears began to flow from my eyes.

"Karma, you passed out. You must have been exhausted; the paramedics said you were dehydrated and covered in blood when they found you by the side of the road." Kayren sobbed again. "I'm so sorry, Karma, but you missed their funeral."

At first I couldn't talk. I truly didn't know what to say. I was crushed, hurt. It felt like my world was over. I felt like I had died with my mother and father that night. Maybe I had, because death was the only thing I felt in my heart.

I wanted to kill. I didn't know why; I just knew I wanted any bad person dead! And then, through my tears, I started to see some things I hadn't noticed before. "Sisters, I'm so glad y'all came to see me and I love y'all. But I need to talk to Steven. Alone."

One by one, my sisters hugged me and left the room. Steven sat down beside me and took my hand. "How can I help you, Karma?"

"I don't know why my father was sad," I began, "and I don't know why he wanted to kill himself. But I do know he wanted me to continue the tradition and kill the bad people in our world. And also to take care of my sisters. I plan to do all of that. What day is today?"

"It's Thursday," Steven said softly.

"OK. Today is Thursday. I should get out the hospital tomorrow. That's Friday. I expect Christian to be ready to tell me who to kill on Saturday!"

Steven's eyes were wide with amazement. He shook his head, but he agreed to do what I'd asked. "Will do, Karma. Will do. But first, I'ma let you get some rest and enjoy your family."

~

What I didn't see was what Steven did on his way out the hospital. He stopped and dropped something into a trash can. It was a syringe, full of a lethal poison.

Christian saw this and asked what it was.

"It was my insurance policy, just in case something different happened when Karma woke up. Thank God I didn't need it. The tradition lives on!"

Chapter 11

Five years later

After my parents' death I trained harder and focused on killing bad people more than I ever did while they were alive. Before he died, my father had put together a book with instructions on how I should train, all the way until I was twenty-five. I must admit that I studied my father's book just as much as I followed the Bible.

I didn't mind killing for God but sometimes I found myself questioning him. Wondering why he would have taken my mother's and father's lives. I sometimes even woke up in a cold sweat, dreaming about seeing them falling from the church tower. Even after five years, I was still having nightmares about that night.

I'd become an even colder-hearted bitch. I never smiled or even laughed. And since the day my parents died, I haven't cried again. Still, I held things down. I took care of my sisters like my father asked me to. When they died, we were left with the house paid for, all the cars and two million dollars in the bank.

Steven helped us; he arranged for Kayren to legally adopt all of us when she turned twenty-one. Young as she was, she was nervous about all the responsibility but stepped up to the plate. She made sure we all ate, went to school and behaved. I was very proud of her. She even allowed me to train as much as I wanted to with no problem.

Steven was in my life more than ever, helping me get my life back together. He was there for my sisters every day. He was also assigning missions for me at least twice a week. Steven basically became a father to me; Christian became my brother.

Even though I questioned God, I still studied his word with Christian like my father had wanted me to.

So eight years later, my sisters and I were doing well. By the time Kayren was 29, she was a lawyer at one of Miami's top law firms. She had four beautiful kids. Unfortunately, her husband was that bastard Kale. I'd hated it when they got married but maybe he remembered what I'd done when he tried to mess with her before. Anyway, he wasn't violent with her anymore, so I had to bless their wishes. Santana had always wanted to be a pastor and finally fulfilled her wishes; with Steven's help she took over a small church. The twins, Sariah and Kariah, were in college at the University of Miami, where our mother had taught. Tennessee hadn't wanted to go to college and ended up working at a nice bike shop that her boyfriend owns. People think Tennessee is the bad one in the bunch because she's tatted up everywhere, but actually she's one of the good ones.

Destiny is twenty-three. She was placed in a good home for people with disabilities like herself. I've been seeing her every day since she went to live there.

Last but not least is me. I'm twenty-one now and mean as ever. Even though I graduated with a 4.5 GPA and was offered a full scholarship to Harvard, there was no way in hell I was going to leave my sisters. So I started my own night club, where I make nice money. My friend Kayla is my assistant manager. She helps me with everything. She is and always was my best friend so I didn't mind at all letting her basically handle all my business. The club was making twenty-seven thousand a month so I didn't mind at all paying Kayla sixty thousand a year to run it. Kayla also has a company car and health care, and got a ten-thousand-dollar bonus for Christmas. She was set, and so was I. All I had to do was go to the club whenever I wanted—and drink. Kayla took care of my finances as well as running the club.

I, on the other hand, had become pissed with the world. I was getting bored with just killing and I decided to put my training to more profitable use by blackmailing people, with a side business of robbing big companies. I had to do whatever I could to keep my mind busy. I also picked up a couple bad habits: drinking and smoking weed.

Steven knew everything about me and tried to get me to change but he must have realized I wasn't going to. So he just asked me to promise him I would go to church and study with Christian, just like I did as a child. It was easy to make that promise because it was the same promise I'd made to my father that long time ago. I never lost faith in God; I just had to live my life the way I want to.

Also following what my father had laid out for me, my training became extremely intense. I worked and practiced harder and harder. I felt like I couldn't train enough. I was running a marathon every other day, boxing two hours a day and another two hours for martial arts. After miles of swimming each day, I practiced my shooting and knife skills for hours. I also worked on being completely quiet and unnoticed as much as possible.

I didn't have time for a boyfriend, school, friends or any of that shit. All I had time for was my sisters, killing, and becoming an even better killer than ever. It's not too much bragging to say my skills have advanced times ten since I was thirteen. Now at twenty-one, I really have nothing to lose. My sisters and the thought of protecting them is what kept me alive. Still, I didn't care if I lived or died.

Steven says that thought alone makes me a perfect killer. The true fact is that I'm the best killer in the world. I wasn't proud of it but I also never regret anybody I have killed. I don't keep a tally; that's Steven's job. I just know that it's been over two hundred people. I've killed lawyers, pastors, teachers, priests, bankers, and more. All deserved it. All of them needed to die. I didn't pick them to die, God did.

I didn't trust anybody but Steven, Christian and my sisters. Whenever one of my sisters dated, I checked out their boyfriends and basically went on the date with them. My sisters never complained about this; they just didn't know I was there, watching everything. But I was. I'd promised my father I was going to take care of them and that is exactly what I did.

Even though I killed, robbed, blackmailed, smoked, drank—and even got some male attention from time to time—I still considered myself a Christian. Of course, if people knew what I did, they would think I was nowhere near a Christian. I do know that I prayed every night, went to church and gave to the poor as much as I could. I also knew no one is perfect and that we all have sins. I just had a lot. I didn't judge myself even though my job was sometimes to judge others. I live like I'm supposed to! I don't feel like I'd changed since I was a kid other than a few of my habits. One change was that now I didn't give my victims the chance to ask God for forgiveness before I killed them. Instead, I would just kill them, without wasting any time. I felt like if God wanted them dead then it was their time to go, no questions asked.

But even though I was living a fairly good life, I still was letting the drink take control of me. After every kill now I was making a habit of getting messed up at my club, to the point Kayla would have to drive me home. Of course that was after I puked my guts out.

My sisters started to get worried about me. Finally they set up a meeting, which I called a bootleg intervention. As soon as I got into the room, my sisters started jumping down my throat. Santana started it off. "Karma, you're my sister and I love you but your drinking and smoking weed is starting to tear you apart. You come home drunk every night. You barely eat or sleep. Karma, killing yourself is not going to bring Mom and Daddy back."

At first I just let her go on, ignoring her talk, until she said, "Daddy would be very disappointed in you."

That got to me. I stood up, furious. "You don't know the half of it. Daddy would be proud of me! I work damn hard and break my ass every day to make sure my father is proud of me. Just because I drink and smoke doesn't mean I don't run and swim for miles every day and train my ass off for hours; I'm making sure Daddy is looking down from heaven at me with a smile. So fuck whoever thinks otherwise."

Santana shook her head. "Karma, Daddy wanted you to do more with your life then just training, and I don't mean starting a club that's full of sin."

"Fuck you, Santana. You don't know how it feels to be in my shoes and you never will. You don't know how it feels to have Karma's curse."

Tears began to fall from Santana's eyes. "Is that what you think, Karma? That you're cursed?"

"Like I said, Santana. You don't know my life, so stop tryin' to judge it. And you're the only one feeling some type of way about my life. No one else said anything."

Santana looked around the room at our other sisters. "We already discussed this among each other. We were just trying to find a good time to approach you."

I began to look more closely at my sisters, especially Kayren. But I wasn't ready to back down. "I must admit I'm very surprised that my sisters would have a meeting about my life and what the fuck I'm doing. But Kayren, you really surprised me. I thought we could talk about everything and anything. You should have come to me as soon as y'all decided to betray me and talk about my life. Which none of y'all know a fuck about! Fuck all of y'all! You're on your own from now on!" When I walked out that night, I left home for the last time. After that night, it would never be my home again.

I couldn't clear my mind so I started running. For some reason, running has always taken a lot of stress away from my thoughts. I was running through downtown Miami until a brand-new Lexus pulled up beside me. The horn honked twice.

"Karma, I been looking for you. Get in the car!" It was Kayla. She had a phat blunt waiting for me in the ashtray. "You know your sisters are only concerned about you because they care."

I kept running. She cruised alongside me with the window down. OK; if that's how she wants to talk, I can talk. "I know they care," I told her, "but they need to mind their business sometimes."

Kayla started to laugh. "Look who's talking. You won't even let your sisters date a man without you looking up his history and doing a background check on him."

"Yeah, but that's different. I was born to protect my sisters."

"Yes, and they were born to love you. You have to understand that they can't help but love you, so they're going to have concerns. And you got to admit you been going hard on the drink and the smoke, ever since your parents died."

"So you agree with them, Kayla?"

"No, Karma but I got to agree they did have some good points. You maybe don't have to quit drinking and smoking but at least slow down a little. That's all."

I kept up my pace, but couldn't really argue with her. "Maybe you're right . . . ." I turned away from Kayla, into a park where she couldn't follow me.

"Karma!" she shouted after me. "Remember we love you."

"I know!" And for the first time that day, I began to smile.

I climbed over the fence into the back yard and spent that night in the quiet room without ever going through the house. Nobody knew I was there. Quietly working out, I got to thinking about what my sisters were concerned about. I began to realize something. It was time for me to get my own place. Not because I was mad at my sisters but because I felt that Kayla was right.

If I want them to be out of my business then I'd have to give them some space; let them live and not be in their business so much. Since they're all grown I have to let them live a little, just like I wanted them to let me live, too.

The next morning I checked out a house I'd seen on my runs, just seven blocks away. I didn't want to move too far off. I could still keep an eye on my sisters but I wanted to be far enough to give them some space. The realtor got a gleam in her eye when I told her I'd be paying cash. For my eight hundred thousand dollars I got two stories, four bedrooms and a lot of space for my training. I even had an indoor pool. I was very content with my new home.

My sisters might have thought I'd moved out of spite, but honestly it was time. I moved all my things out of the house where I'd grown up. I took with me all my weapons, training gear and any information about what my father and I had been training for. I left no evidence of anything, other than some family pictures. If not for word from my sisters' mouths you would have never know I'd ever lived there.

At first I put all my stuff in storage and took a week, with help from Steven and Christian, to build me a secure underground room. It would be my office and storage for my weapons. Then came the hard part, which deep down I'd always known I had to do. I stopped drinking and smoking weed. That just made it easier to start training harder than ever and focusing on God. I knew I had to become a better person, for my sisters if not for myself. I spent three weeks on perfecting my new house into the home I wanted it to be. All this time I was still maintaining the club, killing on God's orders, and also black-mailing a crooked police officer. All this time I forgot that, except for Destiny, I hadn't talked to any of my sisters for almost a month.

I was just starting to think about them when I heard a knock on my door. Kayren greeted me with a huge hug and a smile. "Karma! You know we miss you!"

I was so excited to see her that all I could do was smile. "I've missed y'all too!" I took Kayren on a tour of the house, showing her everything I'd done to it. Everything except the underground room, of course. Kayren was amazed and very impressed with how much progress I'd made in just three weeks. After all the hugs and the "I've missed you," it was time to talk seriously.

As the big sister, Kayren wanted the first words. "I know you were disappointed in me for how we all confronted you. But you must understand that I was stuck in the middle. If I would have told you in advance, they would have thought I'd betrayed them. I thought you would have been more understanding. I'm sorry if you feel I betrayed you in any way. I love you and I always will!"

I hugged her tight. "I love you, too, and the past is the past. You should be glad to know I don't smoke or drink anymore. I'm also trying to get more in touch with God."

Hearing that, she hugged me even tighter. "That's great. I'm so proud of you!"

"That means a lot coming from you!"

Then Kayren let me go and backed up a step. "I gotta go and pick up the kids, but I'll be visiting all the time, now, li'l sis. I love you!"

"Love you too . . ." I was about to give Kayren another hug when I noticed a bruise on her arm. "What happened there?"

Kayren looked away and said, "Nothing, um . . . I was playing outside with the kids and I slipped and fell."

I wasn't about to make her feel bad, so I went along. "Oh, OK. Well, girl, don't play so hard! Remember, you're not the young Kayren anymore. L.O.L!"

She put on a brave smile. "I'll be more careful."

Even before Kayren got to her car, I was planning my next move. I knew her ass didn't fall. I knew there had to be more to it, so of course it was time to investigate. I decided to pay that punk-ass Kale a visit.

The next day, when I knew Kayren would be at work, I went to her house and knocked on the door. When Kale answered it, I greeted him with a punch to the face that made his nose bleed. "What the fuck you hit me for?"

"Bitch! You know why. I hit you because you put your nasty hands on my sister. I told your ass when I was a little kid that if you ever touch my sister I would kill you. But since you're her husband and the father of her kids, I'ma let you live."

He didn't know what to say about that.

"What I am gonna do is mess you up."

Kale screamed, "Karma! Stop! Please! I'm sorry! I lost my job and it's been hard for me. I started drinking heavy."

He was on the floor by now; I stood over him with my fists ready.

"Kayren and I started arguing one night," he said, "and I accidently hit her."

When he said "accidentally," I got ready to punch him again.

"But I swear I didn't mean to!" He was starting to cry by now. "And I swear it'll never happen again! I'm soooo sorry, Karma! You gotta believe me."

"I believe you," I told him. "But you still have to take this ass-whippin'." I began beating Kale's ass. I beat Kale's ass like he stole something. I didn't give a damn why he'd hit my sister. The point was that he did hit her. After I whipped his ass I left him with a thought. "If you touch my sister again, ever, I will kill you! And you better not say shit to my sister about me whipping your ass either, or I'll come back and whip your ass again!"

I left kale with a busted nose, five bruised ribs, two black eyes, and a few knots on his forehead. He was lucky he caught me on a good day, or I would have messed him up some more.

After having this lovely conversation with Kale I began to realize I still needed to protect my sisters, just like I'd promised my father I would. I'd only been out of Kayren's life a few minutes and Kale already felt he could put his hands on her. But hell, no. That was not going down!

Next stop was Steven's house for our weekly confessional meeting. "Forgive me, Father, for I have sinned. I've killed seven people this week."

He wasn't expecting that. "Seven? I thought you only had four to kill."

"You're right, I did. But a lot of crazy things were happening at Destiny's group home, so I had to handle it. I killed the extra three because one was raping clients, one was abusing clients and the last one was feeding the older clients poison so they would die off early. I don't like to kill without God's permission, but I had to do it quickly. See, that's where Destiny wants to stay. And I refuse to let her stay at a place with those type of people. So the rapist: I killed him and fed him to the guard dogs at that old garage over there on Sixth Street. I killed the abuser by abusing his ass just like he'd done, and then drowning him in the Miami River downtown. Last but not least, I killed the third one, the poisoner, by pushing her off a twenty-eight story building."

I had no idea then how that last bit of information might have hit Steven. Sounding as sincere as he could, he replied, "In the past, your killings were quick. You must still have a lot of pain in your heart from your parents' deaths."

"No disrespect," I told him, "But don't talk about my parents. I don't want to hear it! I kill this way because I want to."

"OK, Karma. I understand."

"Good. So what's my next mission?"

"There's this man named John. He's a big-time captain for the Police Department. He's earned a lot of awards. Many people admire him, but little do they know, he is a child molester. His interest is little boys. He also has killed or sent many innocent people to jail. I want you to kill him, but not in the usual way. I want you to disclose all his bad habits to all the people who thinks he is such a good man. The perfect time will be exactly a year from today. He'll be honored at a formal ball."

"Next year?"

"Yes, next year. I want you to get close to him. Allow him to trust you. He has a son named Phillip. He's a great kid and happens to be the same age as you. I want you to get into a relationship with him. Let him meet your family like you truly love him; make him love you enough to tell you more of John's dark secrets. I also want you to find John's secret safe. We know he has at least ten million dollars in unmarked bills he's stolen from evidence. I want you to find that money and take it. Whatever you take, you can keep half. I will safeguard the other half."

"So I gotta get close wit' a punk-ass and all?" Sometimes I liked to talk like this, forgetting my education, just to see how Steven would react. But he let it pass. "Will this be my only mission for a year?"

"No, Karma, it won't. But this killing must be your main focus. I will have small missions for you, but I want them all to be quick deaths. Not anything that will take your focus off the main mission. Or attract too much notice. Understand?"

"Yes, sir, I understand. So when do I start?"

"Today! Philip will be at the park at three thirty today for his normal run."

"He likes to run? I like him already!"

"Good. He is what you need to focus on the first month or two. Don't put a lot of attention on John. He's a very paranoid person, so act like you're so in love with Phillip that you barely know his father exists. Oh, and I want them to know your real name. John will investigate you, but he won't find anything but an athletic girl with an extra-clean record and honors in school. Then after you kill John, wait a few months before you dump Philip. Understand?"

I understood and I told him so.

"It's three now, so go get ready to meet Phillip. And good luck."

I must admit I was uncomfortable about meeting Phillip. I basically had to get a boyfriend and be with him for a year. Killing a stranger is way easier than being with a man for a year and acting like I'm falling for him. I don't like that lovey-dovey shit. I'm too hardcore for that in my real life, but a mission is a mission. Plus, I remembered, I stood to make five million for this. So lovey-dovey it is.

At the park, I spotted Phillip right away. I was glad to see he was good looking; that would make the mission a little easier. I intentionally ran into him and pretended the bump made me fall.

Phillip reached his hand out to help me up. "I'm sorry about that. Are you OK?"

"Yes, I'm OK," I said, taking his hand. "Just didn't see you when I was running." I got up, brushed myself off and turned like I was going to start running again.

"Wait! Um . . . My name is Phillip."

I stopped, turned, and gave him my brightest smile. "Hello, Phillip. I'm Karma."

He began to stare into my eyes, which I have to admit are beautiful! "You are so pretty. I've never seen you around here before."

Perfect. He was taking the bait. I smiled again and looked down, as if I was blushing from his comments. "I usually run in my neighborhood but I decided it's such a lovely day, I'd run in the park."

Phillip returned my smile like he believed in love at first sight—and had just found his true love. "I know you must get asked out a lot, but I feel extremely bad about making you fall. So I want to apologize. By taking you to dinner."

I looked up and smiled again, turning the brightness up another notch. "Um, I don't know . . . ."

Phillip's eyes were an enchanting light brown, I noticed. "Please," he said.

"I promise to have you home at a decent time."

"OK, I said," fluttering my eyelashes at him. "One date. But after that, you've repaid me for my fall."

"OK! Great!" Phillip was grinning like a kid who'd just been told he could have anything in the candy store. We exchanged numbers and decided on a lovely restaurant in Miami Beach. He would make reservations for eight o'clock.

I must admit that Phillip was fine as hell. He was tall, had a beautiful smile and muscles like he worked out a lot. Still, I was focused on my mission and told myself I couldn't fall for this guy. That night, he wined and dined me, and I was impressed by his charm and intelligent conversation. I must admit he swept me off my feet. Still, I was playing the role. I knew what my goal was: it was to kill his father! Nothing more, nothing less.

After a lovely dinner we took a nice walk along the beach. We talked for hours and hours. For a sec, I forgot I was on a mission instead of a real date. But then I told myself not to worry about it so much: as long as I didn't forget my mission, I could still enjoy myself. After our date, Phillip pleaded to see me again. Of course, I said yes. He was interesting. After that first night I was actually looking forward to seeing him again.

I began to see him every day. When I wasn't with him, we talked on the phone for hours. We spent most of our time together until finally, two months later, Phillip asked me to be his girlfriend. That's when he said he wanted me to meet his father. I was soooooooo happy!

Philip thought it was because he'd asked me to be his girl. He didn't have a clue that I was happy 'cause I was about to meet the man I was going to kill. Even though I had numerous dates with Phillip, I was glad to realize I hadn't fallen in love with him. But it was clear he was in love with me.

He would do anything for me. I had him in the palm of my hand like I wanted. And now the day came: it was time to meet John. I'd been waiting on this for two months. I put on a nice outfit that made me look both respectable and intelligent. At his house, was greeted with warm hellos and a delicious meal that Phillip cooked himself. He did the works. He served me and his father green beans, mashed potatoes, ham, turkey, candied yams, mac and cheese, corn and steak.

I was tearing that food up, enjoying my meal, until John spoke up with that firm cop's voice. "So I hear you're an assassin."

I choked on my food, while slowly reaching for my gun. I was seconds away from killing John, and Phillip too, right on the spot.

Then Phillip began to laugh. "Dad, please stop joking with Karma."

I began to laugh, maybe a little bit too hard, while slipping my gun back into its safe spot. Little did they know I'd been about to kill both their asses, in ten more seconds, without a second thought.

"So, Karma, all jokes aside: tell me about yourself."

"Well, there's not much to tell," I answered, "Except that I own a night club; I have my own house; I like to exercise; and I'm the youngest of seven kids. All of us are girls."

"What about your parents?"

"They died in an accident, years ago."

I looked down at my plate; I'm sure the hurt showed in my face. Even talking a little about my parents still affected me.

John could tell. And I could tell he wanted to push my buttons. "So how'd they die? They must have been some careless parents to leave seven girls alone in this world."

Phillip glared at his father. He was as angry and shocked as I was that he could just come out and say that to me.

John gave his son a calm look. "What? I'm just asking a simple question."

I said, "I'd rather not talk about it. Ever. Excuse me; can I use your bathroom, please?"

"Yes, sure. It's down the hall to the left."

On my way to the bathroom, I made sure neither John or Philip could see my anger. Locking the bathroom door, I pulled out my gun, cocked it, and made up my mind I was ready to go kill John's ass. Right now. Fuck this mission and the cash.

I'ma kill these muthafuckers right now! Holding my gun close to my face, while boiling with anger, all I could see was red blood pouring out of John's body.

Two soft knocks broke into my thoughts. "Karma, are you OK?" For some reason, Phillip's voice brought me back to reality.

"Yes, Phillip. I'm OK. Be out in a sec." I uncocked my gun, put it away again, and unlocked the door. I forced myself to stay calm as I sat back down at the dinner table. I didn't want John to see my weakness. In just one conversation I knew not just that I was going to kill John, but also how I would do it. I was going to make sure he suffered a slow, painful and humiliating death if that was the last thing I do.

Even though I was completely focused on killing John and finding out where his stash was, I was completing other missions for Steven, meeting Christian for Bible study, keeping an eye on my sisters from a distance, managing the club, training every day and also having a relationship with Phillip. He was starting to grow on me, which was different. I'd never really cared for a man before. I'm afraid I started to actually fall in love with him. We'd been dating for five months and finally he confessed to me how he truly felt about his father.

It was a rainy night, so we decided to get a few movies and some drinks, kick back and get drunk. I didn't drink like I used to, but I still got my drink on from time to time. While the alcohol was loosening him up, I wanted to have a deep conversation with Philip. I hoped to get him to open up about his father and possibly get him to tell me things he wouldn't tell anyone else. I knew that for him to do that, I would have to tell him some private things of my own.

"Phillip I usually don't speak about my parents," I said, handing him a fresh drink, "but I wanted to explain my emotional reaction when your father asked about them."

Philip was already pretty drunk. He slid closer to me, listening like he'd been waiting for me to speak about it for a long time.

"Eight years after my parents died, I've never spoken about this, but I feel like I can trust you. I just ask that, after I tell you this, there's no more questions"

"I understand. And you don't have to tell me if it's going to make you sad. I hate to see you sad, always want to see you happy." He gave me one of those big, sincere, drunk smiles. So I was confident that he would be ready to open up when it was his turn.

"It's OK. You need to know this. My father was depressed for a couple of months after we came back from our family trip. I tried my best to make him happy again but I couldn't. I just couldn't, so . . ." I paused as if I was about to cry. I was about to cry. Just the thought of my father's state of mind those two months was almost unbearable for me to talk about.

"He got so depressed that one day. One day after having dinner with my mother, he took her to the top of a church tower and killed her. Then he killed himself. Sometimes I find myself hating him, wondering why? Why?" A tear began to roll down my face. For the second time in my life I felt water from my eyes reach my cheek then fall to my chin. I hadn't planned to get emotional but it just happened.

Phillip slid in even closer to me and gave me a consoling hug. "Karma, I'm so sorry this has happened to you, but you can't let this break you. You got to remember the good times." He was getting teary-eyed himself. "You got to remember how your father was before he killed your mother. And himself."

"Phillip, he killed my family. None of us has been the same since they died."

"You have to forgive him for your own sake. Trust me, I know how you feel—"

"You will never know how I feel!" I lost control and shouted at him. "You'll never know how it feels to find your parents dead and know your father is the reason why. No justice can be done! How do you make peace with that? So please don't say you know how I feel. You will never know how I feel." I began to wipe my tears and try to calm down from the tragic story I had to tell.

Phillip was holding me tighter than he ever had.

"Karma," he said, "I know exactly how it feels to lose your mother by your father's hand. I've never told anybody about this but I got to let you know that I truly understand where you're coming from."

I wasn't expecting anything like this. So I dabbed at my eyes again and listened.

"My mother was a singer. She sang at a lot of different classy jazz joints. She loved music more then she loved herself. She practiced hard and she wrote her own songs. She really believed she was going to be a superstar one day. My father happened to be at one of her performances and fell in love as soon as he saw her. After that he began to bring her gifts. Exquisite gifts like diamond bracelets, necklaces, roses. Even a car! He wanted her so bad that he lied and told her he was a producer and could help her with her career. Dad even bought a little building that he turned into a studio. She believed his every word because of the money he had.

"She didn't have any idea he wasn't a producer; that he was a cop. And that he was getting his money by killing drug dealers and stealing their money. After two years, my mother was deeply in love and she married him. He knew he had her heart. He even convinced her to start doing coke. Told her it would keep her energy up in her performances. She'd never done drugs in her life until she met him.

"He pushed her so hard she was doing over seven performances a week. With the coke he supplied any and every time she wanted it, the life began to take a toll on her. She began using coke more than writing songs or singing. She may have even started to love coke more than her singing. She was using drugs bad but once she found out she was pregnant by my father, my mother stopped the coke and went cold turkey. But after I was born she started smoking weed to take the edge away. She loved me more than her drugs and stayed off them for a long time. She even began singing again.

"At first my father was happy for her but then he began to get jealous to the point he began to lace her weed with heroin. He was her supplier so she trusted the product. She never thought in a million years that he would give her anything bad. After five years of smoking those laced blunts, my mother began to lose herself. She became one of the worst people you could ever meet. Her mood swings became extreme; her depression switched on and off every day. She began to crave my fathers weed, and only his. He was loving it; he knew he had her in the palm of his hand.

"It was on my thirteenth birthday that things fell apart. I'd been having a fun time with my mother and father, but that night I woke up: she was screaming at him, saying he'd poisoned her, calling him the devil. My father began to hit my mother like he always did. Usually she would take the abuse but that night was different. She was fed up. She wanted a better life for me and for herself. She wanted to quit smoking and leave my father.

"She began to pack my stuff and hers and walk to the door. My father grabbed her hand and began to pound her face in. He was yelling, "I will kill you before you ever leave me!" Usually, after a tough beating, my mother would give up and go to her room. But like I said, that night was different. She was fed up to the max. She kept tryin' to leave. Once again, my father started beating her but this time he wouldn't stop. I tried to fight him off of her but he pushed me into the wall. That knocked me unconscious. When I woke up, I found my mother on the floor covered in blood and my father nowhere to be found. I had the phone and was trying to call the police when my father walked in. He grabbed the phone and told the officer that I was just playing, he should ignore the call. He was a cop; why wouldn't another cop believe him? Then he made me dig my mother's grave in our back yard. He told me if I ever said anything that he would kill me, just like he killed my mother. From that day on, I've been living in misery."

I could see through how drunk he was; he was really tore up. His eyes were full of tears. "Karma, with you is the only time I have peace. I feel trapped! I won't ever be able to get justice or revenge for my mother's death. I would kill my father but if I did I would be just as bad as he is. I swore to my mother that I'd never be like my father. So all I could do is pray for his karma to come back on him!" Phillip began to cry out loud, like all his pain was hitting him at one time, like he'd been holding this in for years and finally was able to release it.

I began to feel his pain and feel completely sorry for him. If I was a crier I would have cried with him. All I could do is hold him and say, "Your prayer will come true. Karma is going to give him all the pain he gave your mom and any other innocent people he's hurt. I can tell he's a terrible man. I know Karma is going to get him one day. Promise!"

Phillip held me again and we fell asleep in each other arms. The next morning I woke up to a huge smile from Phillip; he was serving me breakfast in bed. And a question: "Do you really think my father's karma is going to come back on him? You just don't know how many times I've dreamed of him dying and woke up with a smile." Phillip began laughing like he was joking but I could tell he was serious.

I smiled back at him. "Karma is going to kill him, worse than how he killed your mom. I know that for a fact. What goes around comes around."

Phillip began to laugh again until he looked up and saw I wasn't bullshit-ting. I was dead-ass serious.

After that lovely breakfast, Phillip went home and I went for my normal run and four-hour training routine. During my workout, I stopped with a surprising thought. it shocked me to the point that I didn't know how to think or feel. Was I really thinking I couldn't wait to see Phillip again? "I think, I think, I think I might love him."

After all he and I have been through and all the time we've put in together, I must have begun to care strongly about him somewhere between first meeting him and now. Finally I'm realizing it. But as soon as something good begins to happen, something bad always comes to destroy your happiness. That's how it works in my world, anyway.

My phone rang, interrupting my pull-ups. It was Kayren. "I'm doing well, Karma. I was calling to invite you to the party I'm having for the family. I'm ready to meet this mystery man of yours I've been hearing so much about. So please bring him."

"We will be there."

After talking to Kayren, I cut my training short and got some ribs for the grill. I gave Phillip a call and planned to go over to the cook-out at seven o'clock. First, though, Phillip and I decided we'd get together for a few drinks. I could tell he was a little anxious about meeting my sisters; I figured he would calm down if we had a few drinks. We decided to be fashionably late and didn't leave until nine thirty, smiles on our faces and ready to party. About a mile away from Kayren's house I began to feel weird, like something wrong had happened. My heart started beating fast and I had to pull over to throw up. I thought maybe I'd drunk too much. We stopped to get some water. I felt better, so I got back behind the wheel. Phillip assured me that it must have been the drinks that caused me to get sick. I was reassuring myself when I pulled up to find police, detectives, an ambulance and my family clustered all around Kayren's house. My sisters were crying while police asked them questions. I jumped out of my car and rushed straight to the house. Santana stopped me at the door, screaming, "She's gone! He killed her!"

After that, I could barely understand what she was saying.

"Santana! Who's gone?"

"Kayren!" she screamed.

I rushed through the door where the police tried to stop me but I was too fast. When I got into the house all I could see was broken glass and blood everywhere. All over the stairs. In puddles on the floors. I ran upstairs to find Kayren with her youngest child in her arms, both dead from stab wounds. I couldn't believe my eyes.

And now, for the third time ever, I began crying Through my tears I noticed a trail of blood leading to the kids' rooms. I ran to see if they were OK. No. Of course not. Both dead. Also from stab wounds. The blood on the stairs, a cop told me, was from the five-year-old. He'd been trying to run; he didn't make it.

My heart started racing; my mind started going crazy. The scene was so bloody and inhuman that I began to throw up. I couldn't stop thinking it was my fault, that I should have been there, that I was supposed to protect my sister. When a man's hand touched my shoulder, I grabbed it, threw him to the ground and, in a rage, pulled out my gun.

Phillip yelled, "Karma, it's me!"

The cop closest to me yelled, "Put the gun down! Now!"

My mind was so gone I couldn't hear them. I couldn't see Philip. All I could see was blood, Kayren and her kids all dead!

Three different police guns were now cocked, ready to shoot.

Phillip yelled again, "Wait! Wait! Don't shoot her!" Then, calmly, he said, "Karma, you have to come back to us. You have to remember the family you have left."

The tears kept pouring out but my mind gradually came back. I realized that I was pointing my gun at Phillip. I uncocked it and laid it on the floor in front of one of the cops. Phillip took a deep breath, stood up and gave me a big hug. I cried, still in unbearable pain. After a few minutes I'd calmed down enough to look at my sisters and ask, "Where the fuck is Kale!" I knew he had to be the killer.

A police officer replied for my sisters. "We don't know where he's at but that don't mean he's the killer. He could be at work or riding around and don't even know his wife and kids are dead!"

I didn't say a word. I just shook my head and walked away. I stepped into clean, fresh outside air, out of the house and its awful bloody smell, I began to throw up again. "Why? God, Whyyyy! Not Kayren, God, please. Not Kayren!"

I couldn't stop the pain in my heart. The only thing that was giving me peace was the thought of killing Kale. I didn't care why he'd killed her or the kids. All I was concerned about was killing him. He was going to feel more pain then someone burning to death. I wanted to drain all the blood out of his body by torture, then inject the blood back into him so I could kill him again. From now on, he was a dead man walking.

"Karma, let's go." One thing I was grateful for: Phillip was with me. "I think we need to go somewhere you can cool off."

I agreed and let him Phillip drive me to the beach. There, with the noise of the surf drowning it out, I could scream and cry until I couldn't scream and cry anymore. I must admit the screaming eased the pain for the moment, but still, all I could think about was my personal mission to kill Kale.

My cell phone buzzed in my pocket. It was Steven. "I heard about Kayren," he told me. Then, after he'd offered the necessary condolences, he told me what I wanted to hear. "I know where Kale is hiding and I know you want to kill him. All I want to say is, kill him exactly how you feel you need to."

"Yes, sir. I will"

As I ended the call, Phillip asked who it was.

"My pastor he is a great guy," I explained, "and like a father to me. You'll meet him soon."

Steven knew without my saying so that until Kale was dead, I was going to dedicate my life to killing him. No matter what other mission I was on. For the next five days I was completely sick. I couldn't eat, I couldn't sleep, all I could do was think about Kayren. About how she didn't deserve to die. And about Killing Kale. I thought of at least twenty different ways I could torture Kale before finally killing him. I even dreamed of it. I became so depressed that I wasn't working out or communicating with any of my family. I wasn't even talking to Phillip. He called me three or four times a day and all I did was deny the call. I wasn't mad at him or anything; I just wanted to be alone until we put Kayren to rest.

Kayren's funeral was seven days after her murder. I had a coffin specially made so she and her kids could fit together. The coffin was all white, trimmed in real gold. Kayren and the kids were dressed in all white. They looked so peaceful, as if they were sleeping and having the best dream they could ever have had. I knew they were with God now. That thought was the only thing that set my mind at peace.

Steven preached a tearful sermon for Kayren in his big, fine church. Then we buried them in our family cemetery plot. At the funeral I was still distraught but could feel someone staring at me. I turned to my left and there was Phillip, dressed in an amazing looking suit. It seemed like he was glowing, even though he was frowning. I realized that I hadn't seen or talked to him in days. As I turned to walk away from Kayren's grave he approached me.

"Hey, Karma. Are you OK?"

"I could be better," I admitted, "but I'm making it. Phillip, I'm sorry for not—"

"Please, don't apologize. I know you've been going through a hard time. I completely understand."

While he spoke, I grabbed him and held him tight. "Karma, these seven days felt like the worst seven days of my life, and that was because I wasn't near you. I realized you bring me beats to my heart, warmth to my body and blood to my veins. Because of you I'm living again! Karma, I love you."

As soon as I heard those words come out of Philip's mouth I began to feel something I had never felt before about a person. I took a deep release of breath and said, surprising myself, "I love you, too." I was so shocked at the words that just came out my mouth, I couldn't believe what I'd said. I just couldn't believe the fact that I meant it. Never in a million years would I think I would have a love life, or anything more than a quick hook-up. Through all those years, with a couple of men in my life, I would only want affection for one night. I couldn't love or trust a man. Plus, it was hard to believe someone could love me when I knew they would never have the chance to know my true lifestyle. Never know the true me. So instead of loving, I kept my heart to myself. Until the day I met Philip.

Even though I knew I loved Philip and he loved me, I still didn't know if I could trust him. I had to make a decision: either not tell him about me and live a lie or put him to the test; if he failed my test, he would die. I decided to put him to the test.

I would inform him about my plan to kill Kale and see how he reacted. I would also see if he would tell on me or not. I knew that if he betrayed me, I would have to kill him, no matter how much I loved him. I cooked a special dinner for two and invited him over to begin my test. Phillip greeted me with a dozen fresh white roses and a teddy bear. I greeted him with Champaign and smiles, even though I was scared to death about how my test would go.

We lingered over dinner but finally it was time. "Phillip, you know I meant what I said when I told you I love you, right?"

"Yes, I truly believe you!"

"Well, just like you believe me now, I need you to believe me when I say I am going to kill Kale."

Philip looked at me, but not in surprise. He looked as if he'd known I was going to say that. "No, Karma. You're not going to kill Kale."

I stared at my plate, thinking, "Damn. He failed the test already!"

Then Phillip went on. "I will kill him for you."

I waited a moment for the "I'm just kidding, let's have justice serve him." But those words never came to his lips. I even gave him till the next morning and asked him again to make sure.

"Phillip, I know we both were in the moment, but I must ask you again: were you serious about what you said last night?"

Without hesitation, he responded, "Yes, Karma. Don't get me wrong. I'm not a killer, but I will kill for you! I love you and will do anything for you."

"Phillip, I love you too. But I don't want you to kill for me. If anything, I want you to be my alibi while I kill Kale. I wouldn't be able to live with myself if I let you kill him and you got caught and went to jail."

Confidently, Phillip replied, "I won't get caught. I'm not a killer but I have killed before, accidentally, and had to cover it up. I'm not as dumb as you think."

"Accidentally?"

"Yes. Accidentally. I had a friend who was drunk one night. He and I got into a huge fight because he thought I was getting it on with his girl. In reality, I was just being a friend to her because he beat her; that made her depressed. Long story short, he pulled out a gun, we fought and I shot him accidentally with his own gun. I still to this day can't believe that happened. I guess I blocked it from my mind. But I will kill for you. Especially Kale. Remember, I was there to see the pain he put you through. I would kill anybody that put you through pain like that. Anybody."

At first I was speechless. I couldn't believe I'd only known Phillip for a few months and already he was prepared to kill for me. "Phillip, I can't let you kill for me. I refuse to! But I will let you be my alibi."

I recognized the stubborn look on his face. I'd seen it before. But I stared him in the face and his expression softened. "Well, if you insist, then I'll do whatever you want me to. What do I need to do?"

"I plan to kill him two days from now. On that day I want you to come to my house and act like you're with me. I want you to go get food for two, movies from the Redbox, flowers and Champaign. Every place you go, I want you to make sure they have a surveillance camera. We'll go over our date so if the police question us we'll have our story straight."

Philip began to laugh. "It seems like you've done this before."

I began to laugh, too. "I have."

Philip brushed off my last comment and went home to get some rest. "See you tomorrow, baby!"

I lay on my bed and went to sleep. I felt like I could trust Phillip; still, I'd rigged his phone, put a tracking device on him and also planted a mini recorder. I had to be sure I knew if he got any second thoughts. If he decided to tell anyone, I would have to kill him. But for the next two days, I saw that he didn't say a thing. Not to anyone. He kept his word and was at my house on time to become my alibi. I was already set up before he got here. I was wearing all black and had packed a black bag full of knives, guns, electric shock items, a saw, and other tools for torture. I was so anxious to kill Kale.

After getting my story right with Phillip, I headed to where Kale had ended up while his house was an active crime scene. Steven had told me that he was staying at a place his cousin owned, thirty minutes out of town on the edge of the Everglades. I estimated it would take me forty minutes to get there from my house.

I kissed Phillip, jumped into my black BMW and headed out to find Kale and end him. On the way there I thought about Kayren and how she'd had her whole life ahead of her. And her children! Those sweet babies who would never grow up. The rage made me drive faster. Tears began to roll down my face. My heart began to beat faster and for a moment I couldn't catch my breath. I was so upset I had to pull over and calm down.

All my training and experience told me I wasn't acting professionally. I knew that if I went to kill Kale like this, I would kill him sloppy. I wanted to be clear headed. I had to make sure he would suffer like I wanted him to. And, of course, that I would get away clean, leaving no clues.

After I calmed down, I got back on the way. I found myself in front of Kale's cousin's house. I was camouflaged for a night mission with my all-black suit, black gloves and black mask to match. For an hour, I used my scope and long-range listening device to study the scene. It made me sick to my stomach to watch Kale interact with his cousin and his family. Kale, the punk-ass, was playing with the kids and laughing with his cousin everything was normal. I couldn't believe he was acting like nothing had happened. Like he hadn't murdered his wife and his own kids.

I was so ready for them to go to sleep! An hour later, I watched Kale and his cousin put the kids to bed. Kale and the cousin talked another hour. In their conversation I heard the cousin tell him he couldn't keep crashing at his house much longer; that he needed to figure out what his next move would be and what he'd do permanently. Then the cousin went to bed.

As soon as I thought they were asleep I made my move. But before I could actually get into the house, I saw a car pulling up. I hid in the bushes and watched a woman get out, go through the front door, and go into a back room to see Kale while the others were upstairs fast asleep. I snuck in the house and crept up the stairs. I went into Kale's cousin's room and filled it with an aerosol sleeping agent. I might be a killer but I'm not a monster. Then headed to the kids' room. I gave them each a shot of a formula that would keep them asleep, too. Not even a fire alarm could wake any of them up before morning.

Then it was time. I went silently down the stairs to do my business with Kale. He was with the woman I'd seen getting out of the car. They were in the bed. Doing what this sorry bastard should have been doing with his own wife. The mother of his children. I reminded myself not to let my anger make me stupid. I put my training to work and entered the room so quietly they didn't even know I was there. Not until I said, "Get the fuck up."

"Oh, my God," Kale squealed. "Karma!"

"Yes, it's me. Bitch."

116

The woman started to scream.

"Bitch, you shut the fuck up. Unless you want to die right now." At first, I didn't know who the woman was. Then I realized I had seen her before. Sitting on the couch in my sister's house!

"Kale, you are one grimy mother-fucker. This is Kayren's friend!"

"Karma, let me explain—"

"Now it's your turn to shut the fuck up."

With my gun to help motivate her, I had the woman tie Kale up then tape his mouth shut. She was crying and whining, "Please, please, don't kill me."

"Bitch, how many ways do I need to tell you to shut up? You were here to suck his dick, right?" She gave me such a pathetic look, I knew I was right. "Well, get to sucking." Her look got even more pitiful. "Bitch, I said, 'Get to sucking!'" I pressed my gun a little harder into her face. She began to suck his dick. Then I said, "Now bite it off." Now I saw sheer terror in her eyes. "Bite it off, or I will kill you, and I promise it will be a very slow, painful death." She hesitated again, so I shot her in the hand with my silencer then repeated my command. "Bite his fucking dick off or I will kill you." She closed her eyes and bit down as hard as she could.

Instantly, Kale began to shriek through the tape over his mouth. Still, she hadn't completely done the job. So I ordered her to try again. Her next bite took it all the way off. She spit it out with a mouthful of blood and began to puke. After she finished heaving her guts out I shot her in the head.

By this time, Kale had passed out. I rummaged into my black bag to find another formula in a hypodermic—the opposite of what I'd used on the kids upstairs. One good poke with the needle and I woke his ass back up. When I was sure I had his attention again, I got to work. He was tied up and his mouth taped, so it wasn't much of a challenge to beat him to death. I punched him until I got tired so I rested for ten minutes before starting to whip his ass again. After I was finished, Kale was still alive but his eyes were swollen shut, his teeth were all knocked out and his jaw was broken. His face was so bloody I couldn't really see who he was. But that was OK. I knew.

I grabbed the tape and ripped it off. "You have any last words before I kill you and send you to hell?"

His voice was weak but still understandable. "Tell Kayren and my kids I love them!" Then Kale took his last breath. I shot him in the head to make sure he was dead. I untied him and laid him and his girlfriend in the bed as if they were sleeping. I was covered in blood when I got back in my car. I'd covered the seats with a plastic shower curtain so they wouldn't stain.

I drove back to my house smoking a blunt. I felt relieved after killing Kale but for some reason I had an empty, questionable feeling. I couldn't help wondering: why would Kale tell me to tell Kayren and the kids that he loved them, if he'd been the one who killed them? I began to think even harder but came to the conclusion that he'd been so badly beaten and distraught that maybe he was asking God to tell Kayren and the kids that he loved them. He was looking up to the ceiling when he said it. So maybe, in his own way, he was asking for God's forgiveness.

Kale's blood was all over my mask, gloves and clothes. I drove straight to my house to meet Phillip. I couldn't call him because if the cops were to check phone records it would look suspicious. I was especially conscientious about this mission because it hit home. I knew that once the police found Kale dead, I would be the first suspect. I had to be extra careful even with Phillip. He didn't know that I had cameras all over my house, inside and outside, so I could see his every move while I was gone; just in case he decided to call the police or didn't do exactly what I'd told him. Before I went in, I checked out the house to see if any cops were around. Everything checked out clear, so I went in.

My front room was dark. But as soon as I shut the door, the lights flicked on and Phillip was greeting me with a hug. His white T-shirt turned red from Kale's blood covering my body. I don't think Phillip had ever seen so much blood; for a second he was speechless. All I could say was, "I need to take a shower." I went straight to the bathroom, stripped off my bloody clothes and turned on the shower. While rinsing the blood off my body I began to cry, thinking about my parents being dead, and now Kayren and the kids. It was a lot to bear.

Then Phillip stepped into the shower with me. He held me tight under the running water, kissing my fingertips. His hands gave me goose bumps even though the water was steaming hot. Phillip got down on his knees and began to kiss me as if he knew exactly what I needed right then. Then he picked me up with his body-builder's muscles to make love to me. The shower began to feel like rain drops; his kisses felt like I was kissing heaven. He was the best sex I had ever had; that was a huge plus, because it was our first time. For that moment my mind was clear, my heart was pure and my soul was at peace. He wrapped me in a big towel, carried me into the bedroom and gently tucked me under the sheets. Then he climbed in with me. I fell asleep in his arms and had the best sleep I ever had in years. As I was drifting off, all that was in my head was, "I think . . . I think I love him!"

The next morning I slept late. As soon as I woke up I was greeted with breakfast in bed and a ring on my finger.

"Phillip, what is this?"

"It's an engagement ring. Until I met you, I never knew what love truly was. I would live and be miserable if I couldn't be there for you and love you for the rest of my life! I need you like I need air. You're the meaning of my happiness, my importance, my heartbeat. Karma Commander: will you marry me?"

I was so speechless, I couldn't say a word. I had never felt so much happiness fill my heart like this. I began to open my mouth to say yes but before I could get the words out, the doorbell rang.

I threw on a robe and ran to the door, where I saw it was two cops. I had already expected them to come but I was kinda surprised that it was this soon. "Good morning, Ma'am. Are you Karma Commander?"

"Yes, officer, I am."

"Can we come in and ask you a few questions?"

"Yes, sure," I said, "But what is this all about?"

"We should really discuss this inside," the cop said.

"OK." I held the door open for them. "Y'all can have a seat in the living room with my fiancée while I get dressed." Phillip stood in the doorway and silently nodded to the officers. I quickly put on some sweat pants and a workout shirt and hurried back to face the police. I entered the room to see the officers were on their way out the door.

"Excuse me, officers; I don't understand. I thought you needed to talk to me about something."

"You're right, Ms. Commander, we did. But your fiancée has already

119

cleared everything up. We didn't want to waste any more of your time. Oh, and congratulations on the engagement! Phillip, tell your father I said hello."

I gave him my most gracious smile and walked the officers to the door. As soon as they left I gave Phillip a big kiss and a hug. "What did you tell them?"

"I told them exactly what they wanted to know."

"What was that?"

"Kale's friends told him how you didn't like him when he and Kayren got together. And about those times you beat him up. So they wanted to know if you still hated him. I told him you got over all that. A long time ago. Said you were always good with him after he married Kayren."

Wow! Phillip had handled the whole story and I didn't have to say a word. I was so proud of him.

He gave me a big kiss and left to tell his father the news about our engagement. I went back to my room to get dressed for my workout and realized the clothes from Kale's murder were still on the floor. All my pain hit me all at once. I realized that even though I was engaged, I still had been born to kill. I prayed to God and promised him that I would try my best to give karma back to sick people like Kale. I understood that Steven and my father had been right. I was born to kill and that is what I was going to do for the rest of my life.

Even as I was thinking about Steven, the phone rang—and it was him.

"Will you be at church today for your confession?" I guess he knew I would need to after last night's special mission. We confirmed that I would be there in three hours. Not having much time, I got straight to work. I did my pull-ups and pushups, swam as many laps as I had time for, got in some kick boxing and practiced with my knife and guns before doing my run on the way to the church.

Steven was waiting on me. "Forgive me father, for I have sinned."

"Hello Karma. Right on time as usual. How did everything go?"

"It went well," I said. But I realized that wasn't telling the whole truth. "But my mind just keeps wondering why Kale would want me to tell Kayren and the kids that he loved them, if he'd been the one that killed them."

Steven paused for a moment, then said, "I know for a fact that he killed her, because he confessed it to me before he went to stay at his cousin's. So I'm sure he was just distracted and was saying whatever came to his mind."

"Yes, Steven, you're right. I don't know why I keep second guessing myself."

"Probably because you've been through a lot. I know it's hard to kill, knowing it is a sin, but think about it. In the Bible it says that a sin is a sin and yours just happens to be killing. You have a good heart, Karma, and God truly knows that. So don't let your job for him bring you down. You are a good person! Remember that."

Steven was telling me things I needed to hear but I don't think he realized I wasn't ashamed and I didn't regret what I'd done. I just wanted to make sure I'd been giving karma to the right person.

That is now what set my mind at ease. "I will always remember that, Steven, I promise! I have some good but maybe surprising news for you. I'm getting married!"

"Really!" He seemed truly pleased at the news. "To Phillip! I'm so happy for you. I remember when your father told me he was getting married to your mom. He was that happiest man in the world. And I can tell right now, at this moment, that you are the happiest woman in the world. You deserve so much happiness."

"Thank you, Steven! I wish my mother and father could see this. I know that my father would be happy if you gave me away at my wedding. You are like a father to me and I would be so happy if you would. And since Christian is a pastor now, too, I would love for him to marry me and Philip."

"It would be my pleasure, Karma, and it would be Christian's pleasure as well.! You know, you would be his first wedding. He is going to be so excited!"

"I know he will." Now that we had talked about pleasant matters, I had to get back to something I needed Steven's advice about. "But about Phillip: I'm just in between about whether I should tell him everything about me or not."

That must have surprised Steven. Maybe even scared him some. Anyway, I had his attention.

"I already tested him," I went on, "and he passed. But I'm not sure if he can handle the whole truth, especially including me having to kill his father. I happen to know that Phillip hates his father, but I don't think he could ever imagine killing him. The truth is that even if he doesn't agree with me about killing his father, it's going to happen anyway. How do you tell someone that?"

Steven sat still for a long moment before he answered. "Don't just tell him everything right at once. Ease it in and observe his actions. I feel he is the one for you. If he loves you the way I feel he does, then he will love you unconditionally, no matter what."

"You're right, Steven. You're right." I was so relieved that he had just confirmed what I was feeling already. It took such a load off my mind.

"You have three months before killing Captain John. Do you plan to marry his son first, then kill him? Or kill first, then marry?"

"I plan to kill first. If things don't go as planned, and Phillip can't get over the fact that I killed his father, it would look weird for us to get a divorced because of it! L.O.L!"

Steven began laughing. "Karma, you sure do know how to make humor of things. Do you have any questions for me before we end our confession?"

"No, I've already asked what was on my mind. I just want to thank you for being here for me through it all."

"Karma, I love you. I will always be here for you. Since you're now about to be a bride, are you going to stop wearing black all the time? I hate to see such a beautiful bride in a black wedding dress."

This time he made me laugh. "I think I'ma keep dressing in black, but I will make an exception on my wedding day!"

We were both laughing, now, as I left the confessional.

"I'll be keeping in touch about the wedding. And the upcoming funeral for a prominent police officer."

On my run back home I was thinking how I could tell Phillip the whole truth about me? I got home, and noticed that Phillip's car was there, which surprised me. I wasn't supposed to see him until the next day. That made up my mind; I guessed this was as good a time as any.

Chapter 12

John's death won't do us part

Phillip was sitting on the steps, but I noticed he was crying, looking as if he'd seen a ghost. "My father is a sick bastard. I knew he was a piece of shit, but this takes the cake. He has done it this time!" Phillip began to cry even harder. I could feel his pain, though I still didn't know what was going on."

"Please tell me what happened. Maybe we can solve it together."

"We can't change a child molester," he said. I'd never heard such bitterness in his voice.

I pretended that I was surprised. "Child molester? Your father?"

"Yes, Karma, a child molester. I went home to tell him the good news about us and found him in bed with a little boy. Then this sick bastard had the nerve to cuss me out and slap me in the face for walking in on him. I can't believe he's so sick and selfish. He's a fucking police officer for Christ's sake!" Phillip was shaking, he was so upset. "I swear I'm going to kill him!"

I gave Phillip a hug to console him. I needed to calm him down. I sure didn't want him to really go and kill his father before I completed the mission. He'd been lucky once, but without my training I knew he wouldn't get away with it again.

"Phillip. I have something I have to tell you."

"Please don't tell me any bad news. I don't think I could bear it."

"It's kinda not bad news. But it is important news. What I have to tell you is this: I am a woman that kills people who have done wrong things."

He looked up at me, shock in his eyes. He was about to be even more shocked.

"I've killed over a hundred people. Karma isn't just my name; I am other people's karma as well. I was literally born to kill." I could see some understanding on Phillip's face now. After he'd seen me in my bloody clothes, maybe it was making some sense to him.

"But here's the hardest part. My next mission: It's your father. I'm sorry that's why I met you, but I don't regret it."

Phillip was speechless. He couldn't say a word for a long minute. Finally he spoke. "So you got close to me so you could kill my father? Is this love you have for me a lie? How could you do this to me? I love you, Karma. And the whole time you knew you were out to kill my father. You played me."

"No, Phillip. No! Well, at first I did, OK? But then I fell deeply in love with you. Please believe me when I say my love is real. I've never loved anyone other than my family before I met you. Please believe me."

I tried to give Phillip a hug.

"Don't touch me! How do I know you're telling the truth now? How do I know this isn't one of your lies?"

"Because I am telling you the truth. I'm putting it all out there. I swear!"

"This is a lot to take in right now," Phillip said. "I need time alone. I'll call you later." He got in his car and he was gone. I hurried inside to my computer and looked up the feeds from the tracking device and recorder I had planted on him. I heard waves; he'd gone to the beach, the same place he took me when I'd found Kayren dead. That was a good sign.

I figured he had to clear his mind. Even though he was mad, he hadn't gone to his father or the police about my secret. All I heard was him praying to God that I was the one for him, that I wasn't going to break his heart. I put on my headphones so I could lie down and still listen to him. I fell asleep listening to the soothing sounds of the ocean.

I don't know how much later it was that I woke up, hearing knocking through the headphones. I pulled them off; the knocking was also coming from my front door. I ran to open the door and let Phillip in. He hugged me tight and said, "I refuse to let my father's upcoming death to 'do us part.' So let's complete the mission together."

I don't think I'd ever been happier than when I'd heard those words.

"What's the plan?" he asked me.

I grabbed his hand, pulled him inside and told him all about it. After seeing Phillip could accept my plan to kill the father he'd come to detest, I knew we were closer than ever. I decided it was time to be completely honest with him.

I told him everything—except for how Steven gave me my missions. I felt that I should keep Steven's identity to myself for now. Phillip never asked and I never told. I told Phillip everything I'd learned about his father, including the drug money I had planned to steal from him. Part of my plan was for Phillip to get back close with his father, as if he'd come to understand his disgusting ways and accepted them.

At first, it was hard for Phillip to agree to stay cool with his father but he figured playing that part would pay off in the long run. Once I'd laid everything out, Phillip agreed to his part of the mission and went back to stay with his father. As planned, he acted as if everything was cool. He told John about our wedding and John was actually excited about it. Turned out, though, that was because he knew Phillip would move out and stay with me, which would give John more space to do his dirt. Phillip even found his father's cash stash for me. That helped me out because I didn't have to waste my time looking for it while I was focused on other things.

First, I was doing more to help Kayla run the club. To thank her for hanging in there while I was so distracted, I gave her a three week break to go on a vacation with her boyfriend. I spent more time with Destiny. I was also seeing my other sisters every day. I wanted to spend time with them, but also needed their help with my wedding. It seemed they were more excited than I was. I was also completing small missions for Steven, training, studying the Bible, preparing for Christian to become my new mission carrier, and most important, spending time with Phillip and going to church with him every Sunday.

Things were starting to look bright. I even started wearing lighter colors sometimes. Steven was extra excited that I was going to church again, but it also made him worry some. What I didn't realize was that he thought the more I went to church the more I would question whether I had really been destined for this at birth; and if I began to have doubts, I might not go through with the mission. He shouldn't have worried. I truly loved my job, plus everything else in my life, and I wouldn't change any of it for the world. Still, I would listen to him justify my actions. The day before it was time for me to kill John I went to church as usual. I knew Steven was going to speak with me but I didn't know just how enlightening this conversation would be.

When the service was over and the members began to leave the sanctuary, I went off to be alone for a while. I climbed to the top of the tower where, as Steven had told me, my father had killed my mother and then himself. I stared down on the people gathered on the sidewalk to talk before finally going home.

Steven came up alongside me, carrying a pair of binoculars. He told me to look at certain people way down below us. "I want you to know," he said, "that we all sin, every day. Even the church members. You see that woman in the blue with the three kids?"

"Yes, she's the one I see in church Sunday, no matter what."

"Yes, she is here every day. And she's always willing to help. What you don't know is that she's an alcoholic."

"Wow. She don't look like the type."

"They never do. You see the deacon who's always preaching about how it's a sin to be gay?"

"Yes. I see him."

"He had a boyfriend for fifteen years. They just broke up three years ago. Now he's preaching about gays being such sinners because his gay relationship went sour. That deacon been sour ever since. That's why I don't allow him to preach anymore."

"Oh, my. I would have never thought."

"You see that husband and wife that always talk about abstinence and how it's a sin to have sex before marriage?"

"Yes. I see them both."

"They both have a gambling problem. And in order for the wife to stay that man's wife she had to become a swinger. Her husband just had a baby by another woman."

"Are you serious? I would have never thought."

"Yes, I'm serious. A hundred percent of the members here are sinners. They judge, but have their own problems. They get to live because God knows that their sins are only hurting themselves." Then Steven stopped and waited for me to put down the binoculars. I looked at him, knowing he wasn't finished. He went on, "These other people out here that are molesting kids, killing innocent people, killing for greed, beating their woman till you can't recognize her, Hurting Gods kids: those people deserve to die and go to hell. You are here to make that happen. Remember that!"

"I know, Steven. I feel it is a pleasure to kill for God. I know I'm doing the right thing."

Steven leaned over to hug me. "As long as you understand."

I smiled at him. "I do. I'm living to learn and learning to live." As I said that, something popped into my mind. "I never asked you this," I said, "but I was wondering: what were my father's last words?"

"He said to take care of you and your sisters and that he loved you dearly."

That made me feel even better. "Thanks, Steven. I needed to hear that." I already felt good about what I did for a living but after that conversation it felt like I was more free. And I had gotten an idea. I knew Steven wasn't going to punish these people who do the small sins; but maybe I could. I noticed that most of these people who had deep, dark secrets were also people who had a lot of cash. Maybe I could do a little blackmailing and maybe they would get tired of paying and just stop doing wrong. I couldn't kill them for minor sins but maybe I could teach them a lesson. But I'm just going to keep that in my thoughts, I told myself.

John's death would be tomorrow. I'd hoped and prayed—a little—that John would change but over the year I'd been watching him he actually got worse. So it was no holding back. Time to kill him.

Next morning I ate a big, well-balanced breakfast and worked out all day as usual. Then I got ready for John's big party. I put on a short, sexy black dress with the heels to match. Since it was a fancy gala I decided to dress it up and added the diamond necklace and earrings. Philip picked me up in a brand-new black Jaguar. He told me his father had given it to him as an engagement present.

I couldn't stop staring at Phillip. He looked so good in his black tux, black hat, black gaiters and a fresh haircut. He was looking so delicious, like a caramel Hershey almond crunch bar. They don't even make those, so yes, he is one of a kind. We both looked so good and we both felt some tension about what we were planning to do. And so we decided the best way to relieve the stress would to be to make love in Phillip's new car. We were spontaneous like that.

I think the idea of us killing together, as true partners, made us horny.

When we'd put ourselves back together, we got to John's house, where he was waiting and seemed so happy. He believed he deserved the honors and award he was about to get, because of all his hard work. Sick Bastard.

Still, we smiled as if we were happy for him, too. "OK, y'all; it's time to go.

We don't want to be late."

"Wait, Mr. John. I think we should make a toast to your success!"

Phillip agreed. "Yes, father. You worked so hard, that's the least we could do!"

John smiled. "You're right, son. And now my new daughter-in-law." I got three glasses. One of them was special. Just for him. His drink was mixed with a slow-acting poison that would give him just three hours to live, and then wouldn't show up in an autopsy. As soon as we toasted—to his death, if only he knew—it was time to go.

The police department had a decked-out limo waiting for us. Fifteen minutes later it delivered us, right on time. The ballroom was beautifully decorated, with crystals everywhere. Everyone was dressed to impress. The food was awesome and served to perfection.

Phillip and I sat back, ate our dinner, got our drink on and waited for the deadly show. For two hours we laughed and talked about John's accomplishments. Then it was time to show a tribute to Captain John on a big video screen. Everyone sat back to watch, expecting the video was going to show John's hard work and accomplishments during his time on the police force.

Just a minute or two in, the audience started to gasp at what they saw. The video was showing all the dirt I had recorded him doing. The video showed him at a crack house collecting protection money from dealers; footage of him raping a little boy he'd met through a police program for poor kids; and to top it off, long close-ups of documents that proved he had been stealing from police evidence rooms, how he had blackmailed innocent people and even that his wife, who supposedly had run off with another man, was really buried in John's back yard.

From stunned silence, the crowd slowly started to whisper, watching John in disgust and disbelief.

John panicked. He pulled out his police-issue revolver and grabbed the person closest to him as a hostage. It was the mayor's wife. He started dragging her toward the door.

In a room full of police, officers by the dozens pulled out their gun and yelled, "Captain, Put the gun down!"

John yelled back, "Hell, no. I'm getting the hell out of here, and if y'all

128

want this bitch to live, then you'll put your fucking guns down."

The crowd of cops began to lower their guns.

"OK, John," one of them said. "We don't want nobody to get hurt. Just put the gun down."

John wasn't about to give up. But a moment later, he started choking and grabbing his neck. He let go of his hostage and tried to limp out the doors behind the head table. Three minutes later, he was lying on his "Congratulations" cake, dead. The plan had worked out so perfectly that when he fell dead I wanted to jump up and give myself applause! I literally wanted to start clapping for my damn self but all I could do was sit there and act as if I was sad. Phillip did a sneaky pat on my back to congratulate me, then ran to his father as if he was concerned. I promise that John's testimonial dinner was the best party I have ever gone to. John had done so many people wrong that nobody asked any questions when the coroner said it looked like a stroke. I heard that maybe ten people showed up at his funeral. I wish I could have been there to piss on his grave.

Still I couldn't. I had to attend Kayla's father's funeral. He died of cancer. He was a good man and I felt it was my duty to attend his funeral. After John was out of his life, Phillip seemed so much happier, and was five million dollars richer! John had more money stashed than what we'd thought. I was able to give Steven the five million he was expecting; Phillip had five million plus two hundred thousand from John's life insurance; and I had five million of my own.

Everything was going great. I turned ownership of the club over to Kayla. We cooked up a deed that made it seem she had bought the club from me with the three hundred thousand she got from her father's life insurance. I moved my sister Destiny into her own house next door to mine and paid for a live-in care provider. I also gave all my other sisters money to help them fulfill their goals and pay off their bills.

Phillip and I started a home for abandoned kids. First one in was the boy we'd caught John abusing. We arranged for a therapist to help him get over what had happened to him. Finally, working together, we built a shelter for the homeless. I also went on with my blackmailing plan. I was happy to find out that ninety percent of the people I blackmailed got the message and changed their ways. Phillip even built himself a gym and became a professional trainer. Since we were doing so much, we had decided to wait a year, then have the wedding. People thought this was because of John's horrible death.

A year later, and a week before the wedding, I was almost fully prepared. I was happier then I had ever been in my life. I was still completing missions but not as many as I once did. Steven had given me a break to focus more on my wedding. We had thought about having the wedding at the beach, in a park or by a lake, but I decided that I was going to have my wedding in Steven's church, just like my mother and father did. I really wished they could be here to see how happy I am, but I know they are in heaven and watching over me.

The day of the wedding I went to the beach and talked to the members of my family who are now dead. Then I went home to get ready. I had a long lovely wedding dress, personally made, sent from Paris. The dress also had real diamonds all around it that matched my earrings and necklace.

The church was beautifully decorated, thanks to my sisters. My brides- maids' dresses were baby blue; the groomsmen wore baby blue tuxedoes. The seats and floor were covered with white feathers and rose petals tinted baby blue.

After the "I do's" it was time to party. We held our reception on the beach, under the stars. The whole night was perfect. Steven paid for our two-week honeymoon in the Bahamas.

Once we got back it was time to work. I began training again and complet- ing missions. Everything was going well for two years straight until, on one of my missions, I felt sick. I began throwing up before I could even kill my target. I didn't know what was going on; so Phillip advised me to go to the doctor. At first I resisted but after two more weeks of throwing up, I gave up and went.

The doctor checked me out and told me that I was very healthy and ev- erything was fine. I was about to leave when he said for me to wait a minute. "There's one more thing." I sat back down. "It looks like you are three months pregnant."

I was shocked and upset. "What the fuck you mean, I'm pregnant? There's no way in hell I'm pregnant."

The doctor looked at me with a little smile. "I think you just said the most important word. You are sexually active, with no protection. Right?"

"Yes," I had to admit. "You're right."

"Well, you are pregnant. But there's one thing you have wrong. There is no way in hell you are pregnant, but there is a way in heaven you are. And that's because a child is a gift from God."

I couldn't argue with that. I smiled and thanked the doctor.

"Now, you're far enough along that an ultrasound will let you see if you're having a boy or girl. Would you like to do that today?"

"Yes, I need to see this baby inside me; it's still hard to believe that I'm having one." As he connected the ultrasound equipment, I could hear my baby's heartbeat. For the first time, I dropped a few tears of joy. I felt a rush of happiness hit my heart and at that moment it really sank in that I was going to be a mother. I went from being scared to being the happiest woman in the world.

The doctor pointed to a little shadow on his screen. "Congratulations, Karma. You are having a baby boy!"

I couldn't stop smiling. And I couldn't wait to tell Phillip—and Steven—about the upcoming new edition to our family.

Phillip got the news first, and jumped for joy. He was so happy and excited he couldn't breathe. He ran around the neighborhood yelling, "I'm going to be a father!"

Then it was time to tell Steven. I was kind of nervous about telling him because his plan for me was to have a child five years after I married instead of two. But like the doctor said, this had to be all in God's plan. I knew Steven would have to accept it.

I drove to the church and sat down in the confession booth where I knew Steven would be. "Forgive me, Father, for I have sinned. But I also have a blessing!"

"Hello, Karma. This must be very important; you haven't ever came to a confession early before. Is something wrong?"

"Actually, Father, things are just right! I've come to tell you that it's early but we'll have a new addition to the family soon. I am expecting."

Steven paused for a moment. "You're expecting?"

"Yes, Father, I am. And it's a boy!"

"Congratulations, Karma. I'm so happy for you. So I'm going to be a grandfather to two boys. This is such a blessing!"

I looked back at him, puzzled. "I'm only having one."

"I know. But Christian is early as well. His wife is expecting a boy, too."

"This is sooooo great! This means as soon as those babies are born, we can get right back to work."

"Yes, you're right. We can. Now come out of the confessional and give me a hug." With his arms wrapped around me, Steven said, "I'm so proud and happy for you." So I rested in his arms. I knew that since I was pregnant I wouldn't be killing any more for at least five to six months. So all I had to focus on was preparing for my son.

I wanted to raise him exactly how I was raised, so I hired contractors to build a quiet room for him, just like mine. I knew my father would have been so happy to know I could continue our tradition with Steven and Christian. I knew that had been his wishes.

It seems like all the preparing and the waiting for our son were over in no time. When it was time for him to be born, my labor wasn't that bad. I actually pushed him right on out with no problems. All that physical training had paid off in a new way!

I named him Myair. The doctor was concerned that he never cried during or after the birth, but I assured him that this was normal in our family; that I had been the same way when I was born.

As soon as Myair was able to walk I started his training. He was going through the steps exactly like I did. Myair was like my clone. Even as a toddler he was powerful and getting prepared to kill, just like I was at his age. He was a sneaky little thing, very nosy. It was hard to keep secrets from him. So Phillip came up with the idea to put on his favorite "Terminator" movie when we needed to do something in private. Myair loved the movie, and he loved Arnold Schwarzenegger's character, so when it was on he wouldn't move a bit. That gave us two hours to talk privately and make decisions without him.

By the time he started school, Myair was becoming very dangerous. Soon it would be time for his first kill. I even took him on one of my missions to show him how it's done. He was also spending time in Bible study with Christian's son, Chris. Soon Chris would be following his father's footsteps, just like Christian was following Steven. Myair was so excited to be the next generation, following in his mother's footsteps. I loved my son and he loved me.

132

Surprisingly, Phillip wasn't mad about this. He didn't disagree about his son being raised to be a killer. After how he'd seen justice done to his father, he actually liked the fact that his son would grow up to do justice to others who needed it. And so we all were one big happy family. Everything about our lives was great.

Chapter 13

A mission to remember forever

One night at dinner time the phone rang. It was Steven. "I need to talk to you as soon as possible."

I told him we were having dinner, but that I'd be over as soon as I could.

Whatever Steven wanted to talk to me about was major. He never called me at this time of night. The thought drove me to the point that I stopped eating, excused myself from Phillip and Myair, and rushed right over.

Steven greeted me, saying, "I hear Myair is doing great with his training, and learning the Bible very well, too."

"Yes, sir, he is. I'm so proud of him."

"That's good. That's good." Then Steven got down to business. "I called you because I have a very special mission for you. This is going to be one of the biggest missions you ever completed. It means more to me than any mission you have ever been assigned to. I need you to understand its importance."

I was eager to hear more. "What is the mission?"

"I need you to kill a pastor for me."

"A pastor?"

"Yes, Karma, a pastor."

"What has he done?"

"He has killed. Also, he has preached for his own benefit and not God's. He is a very sneaky; he will try to say anything to stop you from killing him. It's very important that you don't listen; just take him down. You know I wouldn't ask you to kill a pastor if it wasn't very, very serious."

"I trust you, Steven. This pastor is now a dead pastor walking."

Steven nodded, pleased that I was so excited about the mission. "You will need your fake passport, because you will have to go to the Dominican Republic to kill him." He went on to explain that I had to act fast. "I'm just finding out that this pastor has left here for the island but he'll be returning in three days, so I need you to leave first thing in the morning."

I didn't think twice. And I didn't think at all to question Steven about the mission. I just went home and began to pack for my trip. I told Phillip about it and how soon I had to depart. He understood, and we made sweet love that night, like we were trying to make another baby. The next morning I kissed my son and hurried to catch my plane. The flight was peaceful. I relaxed and looked over the documents that told me every move this Pastor Carson would make. I was in a rush to kill Carson so I could get right back to my family.

As soon as I landed, I realized I'd been there before. This was the place where we as a family took our last vacation before my father killed my mother. It brought back so many memories as I walked the beach where we'd once played and laughed as a family. I even remember swimming to a small island offshore, which happened to be where I had to go to for my mission.

I could have taken a boat, but I decided to swim for old times' sake. In the water on the way across, I recalled the good memories of swimming alongside the boat, my father pushing me to keep going, and smiling with pride about me working so hard. The thought filled my heart with warm happiness. For a second, I felt as if Daddy was there, right beside me. As I reached the island I imagined my father giving me a hand, helping me out of the water and telling me, once again, how proud he was of me. It was like I could feel his hugs and heart again.

I had two hours before it got dark so I found a secluded spot to relax and thought about when our family was a whole. I imagined how it could have been, right here, if Kayren and her kids, my mother and my father were all still alive. I imagined Kayren on her beach towel reading, my father and mother hugged up, Kayren's kids playing with Myair, Philip on the grill, and Kayla and me laughing and making jokes. This vision felt so real that I could hear the laughs and smell the food. I didn't want it to end but the sun had set, that tropical darkness had fallen, and I had to put my dream aside. Now I had to accomplish what I'd been sent here to do.

I pulled my gear out of a waterproof bag, dressed in all black, and ran the distance to where I knew Pastor Carson would be. To my surprise, I found Pastor Carson alone, sitting in a chair with his Bible. I sneaked into his church, stood behind him, pulled out my pistol with a silencer, and aimed it at his head.

"Hello, Karma Commander. I've been waiting on this day."

I was so shocked I almost dropped my gun. But I kept myself together, and kept the gun against his head. "How do you know my name?"

"I always knew about you," he said calmly. "Your father, Sincere, told me about you."

I pushed the silencer harder against his head. "How the . . . How do you know my father?"

"He was sent here to kill me fifteen years ago. He had taken y'all on a family vacation as a cover; the trip was really a mission. From Steven."

He knew about Steven? My heart started beating fast and for the first time in my life I was confused about a mission. Even a little scared. But then I thought about it. "You're lying. My father didn't even know about our family's trip! It was a surprise!"

"Karma," he said, reaching back to hand me the Bible he was holding, "I have something for you—"

"Time's up." I shot Carson in the head, killing him instantly. I didn't have time for this shit. I trusted Steven. If he told me to kill Carson, then his ass had to die. Pastor or not. I was about to leave when I heard a thump on the floor. I turned to see what it was; it was the Bible Carson had been holding. I turned again to walk away but then I thought about it. Something in my heart told me to take the Bible so at least I could see what Pastor Carson had been talking about.

It was all lies—I knew it was—but my gut feeling told me to take the book anyway. So I picked it up and tucked it into the bag with the rest of my gear.

I didn't pull the Bible out until I got on the plane back to Miami. Tucked into the book of Exodus, right next to the Ten Commandments, was a letter. I unfolded it and started to read. It looked old; the paper was yellowed and the handwriting was old-fashioned. The letter explained what a lie our long family tradition was. It told me that killing was not what my family was supposed to do. More lies, I told myself. I was in denial until I looked at the end of the letter and saw the signatures: each of my grandfathers and great-grandfathers and last but not least my father's signature. "Sincere Commander," and the date: from fifteen years ago, during that final family vacation.

I was having trouble reading. Tears were forming in my eyes; I turned to look out the window of the plane. Suddenly things started to make sense. I started to put the pieces together. After our trip—after my father signed the letter—he was depressed because he knew Steven had been lying. Then the biggest shock of all hit me.

Steven had invited my father and mother to the dinner that night . . . so he could kill them! My father hadn't killed my mother. He hadn't committed suicide. Steven had killed them both.

I began to feel sick to my stomach. I ran to the plane's bathroom and threw up. I started crying and feeling panicky, like everything I'd thought was solid ground was falling away under my feet. Like I was up on top of a tower and about to fall over the edge.

The whole time I'd been trusting and believing in the man who betrayed my family.

I knew I had to pull myself together. I called on all my years of training and calmed myself down. Back in my seat, I looked back out at the sky and made up my mind what I had to do.

"He is going to die," I told myself. "Point blank." I couldn't wait to get off the plane, but used my time the whole way back to think through how I would kill Steven. I was going to kill Christian, too. I knew that if I killed them both, I would stop this fake tradition. It would all end, once and for all. Christian's son Chris and my son Myair would be able to live normal lives. They would not grow up, like I had, with blood on their hands.

As soon as I got off the plane I was greeted with hugs and kisses from Phillip and Myair. I don't think I'd ever been so happy to see them. But now it was time to get to business. As soon as we got home I popped in the disk with Myair's "Terminator" movie, went into the study and told Phillip everything. I showed him the letter Pastor Carson had died trying to give me. Phillip was totally shocked but he held me and told me everything was going to be OK. Phillip tried to convince me I shouldn't kill Steven because he was a pastor. It would be better for us to move away, he said.

But I was like, "Hell, no. I'm going to kill him for my mother and father. He must die."

Phillip reached out to hold me again, saying, "Give it two days of thought. Then, when you're completely sure, do what you want to do. Promise?"

Phillip was right. Maybe I did need a couple days to clear my mind, and so I promised him. Even so, at the end of that time my thoughts hadn't changed.

I was going to kill them no matter what. The two days did give me time to research some questions that were still unanswered. Ever since I'd discovered that my whole life was basically a lie, I'd been investigating a lot of things that were on my mind. I found out the truth about way more than what I'd bargained for.

It seemed like the only ones I could trust were my sisters, my husband and my son.

When the two days were up, I knew the time had come. I called Steven and told him the mission to the Dominican Republic had been a success but that I had a confession to make. I needed to talk to him tonight, I said.

He told me to meet him at the church at eight o clock.

I kissed my son and put him to bed. I decided to run to the church one last time just to clear my mind. Also, running there would seem completely normal to Steven. On the way, it began to rain. It still felt like a perfect time for a run. As the rain washed over me and I splashed through the puddles, I told myself I didn't want to make Christian or Steven suffer. I just wanted them dead. I wanted to start my life over again.

At eight o'clock on the dot, soaking wet, I walked into the church. Steven was in the confession booth, waiting.

I started the confession a little different than normal. "I hope God forgives you, Father, for you have sinned."

"Karma, I knew you would be too weak to handle the truth."

I was shocked that this fucker got straight to the point.

"I know Carson told you everything, and he was right. God hasn't been telling me who you should kill. But look at the whole story. You have killed murderers, child molesters, all kinds of dangerous people. Doesn't that mean anything to you? Can't you see that you've been making the world a better place?"

"No, I don't see that. I see that because of you I'm a murderer just like the ones I killed. I've been living a lie because of you. And you killed my mother and father! You, Steven."

"I had to, Karma. So the tradition didn't die. I love you, Karma, like my own daughter. I did this for us. For our family."

"Fuck us," I shouted back at him. "There's no 'us.' Ya'll been killing my family for years."

"I'm sorry, Karma, but that's your family's curse. You have to understand that what goes around comes around. Even for you."

"Now for you." This had gone on long enough. I pulled my gun back and fired two shots through the confessional's wooden wall. Then I ran around to Steven's side to make sure he was dead.

He wasn't there. I should have known it wouldn't be this easy. I turned around to see he was running up the stairs. I ran behind him and found myself at the top of the tower. Right where he'd killed my parents. I began searching for Steven and found him standing there as if he was waiting on me. I pointed my gun to shoot.

"You don't have to do this," he said. "We can still continue the tradition."

"There's no tradition! You killed my mother and father! And I found out something else. It wasn't Kale! He didn't kill Kayren! He came to you for advice because he'd hit her again when she found out he was cheating on her. You told him to go stay with his cousin and let things cool down. So you must have killed Kayren, too! And all of her children!"

Steven began to smile.

Then a voice spoke out of the darkness. "No, Karma, he didn't kill your sister. I did." I turned to look and out walks Phillip with a gun pointed at me.

"No. No, Phillip! Not you!" Reality started to hit me all at once.

"Yes, Karma. Me. You see, Steven wasn't the only one who was planning to meet you."

"You've been planning this with Steven the whole time? You fucking bastard."

"Karma, I told you not to kill Steven. I tried to get you to run."

"Fuck all that. Why did you kill Kayren?"

"She knew too much about me. She had walked in on me talking to Steven at the church and heard some info she shouldn't heard and didn't like. So Kayren threatened to tell you about what was really going on. She wanted to break us apart."

"Fuck you, Phillip!"

"Yes, you did, Karma, and very well, I must admit. Now our son can grow up to continue the tradition—being trained by his father."

That thought truly terrified me. "Where is my son?" I screamed.

"He's home. Watching 'Terminator.'"

"You son of a bitch."

"Yes, you're right about that, too. And for the record: I killed my mother; my father didn't. All the so-called proof I had? It was all fake. She found out about the friend I'd killed. She knew it was no accident; she knew I was killing for Steven. She tried to stop me, so the bitch had to die. And now, Karma, you have to die."

~

Phillip pulled the trigger three times. The bullets were so powerful they knocked Karma over the edge and she fell from the top of the church tower. Steven and Phillip exchanged satisfied smiles.

Phillip asked, "How are we going to explain this to the cops?

Steven chuckled softly. "It's simple. The police are going to think Karma and her husband were here at the church fighting, and that things got out of hand. He lost his temper and shot her—but not before she could get a shot off. Her shot hit him in the head."

The smile vanished from Phillip's face. He stared at Steven, his eyes wide. "What?"

One more gunshot echoed above the church tower. With a single gunshot in his head, Phillip collapsed onto the roof. Steven pulled a handkerchief out of his pocket, carefully wiped down the gun, and threw it over the side where Karma had fallen. And then he turned and walked down the stairs.

Chapter 14

An end to a beginning

After making sure Karma's fingers were wrapped around the gun, Steven rushed to her house. He found Myair sitting in front of the TV, watching Arnold as the Terminator. He sat down on the couch with him to watch the end of the movie.

Thirty minutes later the doorbell rang. The police officer on the porch recognized Steven. "Hello, Pastor. I'm afraid I have some very bad news for you."

"Oh, really? What in the world could that be?"

"I'm sorry to tell you that Karma and Phillip Loften just killed each other at your church. Looks like they both shot each other."

"Oh, my God," he said, acting convincingly surprised. "They had asked me to watch their son Myair while they went to pray together, but I didn't know they were having any problems. Are you sure it's them?"

The officer nodded.

Steven began to cry. "Karma was like a daughter to me. I can't believe she's dead. Officer, please: let me break the news to her sisters, and to her son. They wanted me to become his legal guardian if anything was to happen to them; I guess I should take Myair home with me tonight."

The cop asked a few questions about the church, told Steven to expect some routine follow-up by crime scene investigators, and said good night.

Steven closed the door and went back to the room where Myair was still in front of the TV. The credits were rolling at the end of his video. "Myair, your mother and father won't be coming home tonight, so I'm going to take you home with me. We'll get a nice night's sleep and talk about the rest in the morning."

"OK, Pastor Steven. Can I take my DVD with me?"

"Of course you can. And bring a change of clothes with you." Myair ran up to his room to pack his bag.

~

In his guest bedroom, Steven tucked Myair in and gave him a kiss goodnight. Then he went to lie down in bed with his wife. He told her what had happened while he was babysitting Myair. She began crying in disbelief that Karma and Phillip would kill each other. Steven held her tight, telling her everything was going to be all right. He asked her what she thought about having Myair live with them so they could raise him.

She agreed. Steven smiled, satisfied, feeling like the most powerful man in the world. All the complications had been cleared up. First Sincere, now Pastor Carson, Phillip and Karma: none of them could cause any more problems. He was certain now that he could continue the tradition.

Suddenly he heard a door shut. He went downstairs to check on things and found Myair asleep on the living room floor. The case for the "Terminator" DVD was open in front of him, empty. Steven smiled. The boy just couldn't get enough of Arnold and his movie. He knew that tonight had been hard for the boy; it was the first night he'd ever had to sleep without his parents. Steven decided to leave Myair where he was, and lay down on the couch to watch a little TV himself. He reached for the remote and hit the "power" button. As soon as the screen lit up, there on front of him was Karma's face. She was looking right out of the TV at Steven. He sat up, startled, watching closely for the message he knew would be coming. And then Karma began to speak.

"My name is Karma and I'm a serial killer. You see, my father trained me to become a professional assassin. I didn't want this life but I basically was born to kill.

"I'm not proud of my murders I committed but I'm not ashamed, either. I don't even regret what I have done. All I know is that now it's getting the best of me. The murders are starting to become a necessity and I don't know how to let go.

"Through my twenty-five years I've already killed over fifty people. After the tenth one, I just stopped counting. During my journey through life I've also blackmailed and robbed people to get where I'm at. I've killed preachers, judges and boyfriends. All of them deserved it, of course. At least I thought they did. I know you're probably judging me already; but you don't know my story. The only way you might understand me is if you hear this.

"Honestly, I hope you understand. But I know I have a problem. Maybe, hopefully, you can help me solve it. I know you're saying, 'Why would I want to help you after all that has happened?' But you must know that everything is not what it seems. I need you to try to walk a day in my shoes and see where you end up."

On the video, Karma told her whole life story, from before she was born until the day of her death. She even mentioned how, while she was pregnant, she had suspected Phillip of cheating. She'd followed him one night and saw Phillip meeting with Steven, which increased her suspicions. She said she'd first brushed it off, but still she kept the thought in the back of her mind. And that got her thinking about those tape recordings she'd found in her father's car, and in the bottom drawer of his desk, after he'd died. For years, she couldn't bear the thought of listening to them, snooping on what had to have been Sincere's most private business.

But finally her suspicions got the better of her. She dug out those old tapes and listened to them.

At first, she smiled, listening to Sincere and Steven in the confessional, talking about her training. She loved hearing them say how proud they were of her. But then she got to the day her father finally confronted Pastor Carson on their tropical vacation.

Karma's blood ran cold as she heard in detail how Steven betrayed her father. Her attitude turned to hot rage when she heard those last moments of her parents' lives, up on the tower of Steven's church.

When she calmed down, she got to thinking about how grateful she was that her father made those audio recordings. They let her know the truth, even after his death. Then she decided she would do something like that, too. And so she decided to record this video. She copied it onto Myair's favorite DVD, just in case Phillip was in on Steven's scheme. She knew that if Phillip intended to get out of the house without Myair noticing, he would tell his son to put the video on.

Karma had covered her tracks. Her video's last words were, "Son, I love you and will always love you. You are my heart and soul. I want you to forget this life of killing and start a new life. But first, I need you to do me one last favor."

Steven heard these words with a growing sense of dread.

From the TV screen, Karma spoke her last instructions to her son. "I need you to kill Christian and kill Steven." And the video cut off.

Among the thoughts rushing through Steven's head was the realization that if he seen this video, then so had Myair. He realized that, all the time he'd been watching the video, he had forgotten about the boy lying on the floor in front of him. Steven looked down to see that Myair was gone.

Steven reached under the couch and pulled out his gun. On the alert, he began looking for Myair. He heard noises that seemed to be coming from a hall closet. He opened the door to find Christian and his wife, both tied up.

Steven spun around to find Myair standing behind him, fists clenched, staring at him. Steven raised his gun and pulled the trigger. Just a click. He tried again. Click. The gun was unloaded.

Myair opened his hand and dropped the bullets on the floor, one by one. Then from the waistband behind his back, he pulled out a pistol with a silencer.

Steven stood motionless, letting his gun drop to the floor. A tear dropped from his eye.

Four words came from Myair's mouth. "Hasta la vista, baby." Then three shots came from Myair's gun. The first was to Steven's head. To the couple in the closet, he added, "Tradition over, bitch." Two more shots: to Christian and his wife. Myair went upstairs and completed his mission with a single shot to Steven's wife's head. His final task was to pour gasoline in every room and set the house on fire.

Police and fire investigators say the fire was so bad they couldn't identify the bodies. The case is still under investigation.

Myair went home, got his mother's three million dollars, and disappeared. No one has seen him since. Some say he died in the fire.

Christian's son Chris, who was being trained to assign Myair his murder missions, feels he is still alive. One day, Chris hopes, he will be able to find Myair and avenge the deaths of his father and grandfather.

But as far as Myair is concerned, he is on a beach somewhere, far away. You may wonder: how could a five-year-old, even one who had already been trained as a killer, manage to get out of the country without anybody noticing? Well, three million dollars can buy a lot.

Myair had promised himself and his mother that he would never kill again, and he would never return to America unless his aunts were in danger. Even as a child, he understood that his mother had tried to do right, but that things always seemed to go wrong. And that at least two of his victims, Kale and Pastor Carson, had not deserved what she'd done to them. About all the others Steven had sent her to kill? He knew he would never know the whole truth, but suspected other innocent people had been sacrificed to Steven's greed, too. For all her sins, Myair knew even if just the pride of believing she was doing God's work, his mother had finally paid the price.

Guess that was truly Karma's curse.

Postscript

No one must know!

No one must know
that's why my feelings must not show
Still we'll grow something so strong on the low
'cause we both know it's so wrong
but how can something so wrong feel so right
Everytime you in sight
I'm happy and polite
Still it's a sin that I must fight
I think I might
should just leave him alone
then I get a text on the phone
reading, Baby come to my home
so I can massage you
even though
I know
your man is beside you
All I can text back is, This is true
still I want to be with you
Who knew
that something so discreet
could become something so complete
We were not supposed to meet
I was just supposed to greet
and go find my man that was beside my seat
But instead when I met this man
we shared a love that we both couldn't understand
Now my hand
is given to two different men
One was just supposed to be a friend
How will this end?

~

Now we're looking at a menu
I decided to continue
but now we're getting too comfortable
I've stumbled on a love that I don't know how to let go
All I know
is that with you I'm not stressing
so is our love a curse or a blessing
'cause still the matter in hand
is that I have a husband
He is waiting for me to come home
and cook dinner for me and the children
Wow
Is that his best friend that glanced at us eating?
I must continue hiding
It would be hard explaining if he has a full description
I don't think he seen me
Wow that was a close call
then I notice I'm getting a phone call
It's Jason asking where I'm at
and when I'm coming home
I begin to stall
then say I'm with the home girls, we're having a ball
I lost track of time and forgot to call
While my other man looks at me and begins to applaud
I'll be home soon, he replies
Wear something sexy when you reach the bedroom
Yes, baby, Love you too
I'm so caught up, I don't know what to do
I'm 'bout to be lucked up
First I got to change up
Of course what I'm wearing
Jason's best friend was staring

so hard I've should have seen him earlier
Lucky for me Jason left earlier
for work this morning and the dress is new so its nothing familiar
The bigger picture is that
I should be able to get away with it
If I do this love affair is through, THAT'S IT
Awww, SHIT
Please stop touching me
Didn't I say my husband is waiting
Can't you see I'm hesitating
Can't you see I'm fighting your love in the making
Please stop the aggression
and affection
Now I find myself stepping to his house
Kisses quiet as a mouse
He gently lays me on the couch
My phone is vibrating in my pouch
Watch out!
We going for round two
I turned and looked at the clock and its a quarter till two
What will I do?

~

Two a.m.
Got to call my best friend Pam
hope she awake and ready to listen
Hey, Pam, now pay attention
I must tell you my situation
I didn't go home to my children and Jason.

She replies, Melissa are you still messing with that fella?
Oh, I'm sorry, you call him Handsome.
That's his name, but Pam, no time for jokes
I might need to have a story with no hesitation.

Melissa, just say you was with me and fell asleep
no need to tell Jason you were on the creep
like TLC
You right, Pam, I should come up with a story
I'm feeling so stressed
that maybe I should confess
I know Jason will be upset
but maybe I can still save our marriage

Melissa, before you say something you'll regret
the truth is, telling a lie will save you a lot of bad concepts

OK, Pam, this time I will listen
but I shouldn't have when you first introduced me to Handsome

Melissa, just stick to the plan
and all your problems are solved in your complication.

While still in disbelief
that I fell asleep
I took a shower then told Handsome I must leave
Would have left earlier but I didn't want Jason to smell the sex on me

Meanwhile, Pam turns to her side and say
I gotta go, she on the way

I'm rushing home doing ninety-five in a seventy
I know Jason is at home waiting, not patiently
While driving I'm knowing Jason is the best for me
I must stop this affair
and I'm going to start right here
I call Handsome in tears
Hello, I need to make this clear
that our affair is through

I never should have met you

He yells, But Melissa, I love you!
I'm sorry, Handsome, but it was not
supposed to be this way
home is where I'm going to stay!

Please, Melissa, don't let us end like this
I need your touch, I need your kiss

In tears, I say, You will be truly missed
Hung up the phone, rushed in the house
Jason was waiting, without a doubt
Where are the kids?

They're at your mom's house

Please have a seat on the couch
I know its late but the truth must come out
Unfortunately, I haven't been a lady
I begin hesitating

Melissa, keep talking, 'cause right now you sound crazy

Baby, I'm sorry, but I've been having an affair
I've kept it from you 'cause I know you would care

Melissa, are you serious?

In two seconds, Jason went from calm to pissed
Who's the guy you fucking with?

In tears, I say, He is no longer important

Tell me! Jason yells

I'm so sorry, Jason!
He replies, Go to HELL!!
We have a marriage, we have kids!
Jason's temper begins to rise so quick
Smack to the face, I began to fall to the floor
So shocked 'cause Jason's never ever hit me before
As I start to get up and beg him to stay I notice on the floor
Pam's earring

What is this?

What is what?

Jason, you know what the fuck I'm talking about
and before the lies come out your mouth
I was with Pam yesterday morning
when she bought these earrings
and she never came back to our house
Are you Fucking Pam?

Jason replies, No
you just want to justify you being a hoe

You're lying, Jason, you know how I know
'cause over there is also her coat
I begin to choke Jason

He yells, "Melissa, stop!

Jason's mother comes down stairs to see what the arguing's about
Then the doorbell rings followed by a knock
My sure bet: it was Pam but instead it's Handsome and now I'm in shock!

What are you doing here! I shout

Handsome replies, I love you Melissa, and then kisses me in the mouth

I gently push him away while saying, Handsome, stop

Jason reaches for his gun
Since you're here, let's have some fun!

Jason, I told you that him and I are done

Jason cocks the gun while sarcastically saying
So I guess he just here for his health, huh!

I begin to yell

Handsome says, I'm ready to die for love so, OH WELL!

Jason's mother steps between them

Jason yells, Stay out of this, Mother!

She yells back, I can't 'cause that's your brother!

For a moment there is silence

Then Jason says, Mother, you're lying!
While a moment came to me
when Handsome had said he was adopted

Jason says, Mother, this can't be
you always said you only gave birth to me

I know, I know, she says in a plea
I'll explain but first put the gun away 'cause this is getting too deep

Mother, how can this be? Is he the younger or the older?

She replies, Actually, you are fraternal
You was born eleven fifty nine p.m. and he was born at twelve oh-one
different days but still my sons
I was too ashamed to let you know
that I was young with finances low
so the best decision was to let one go

While tears coming from Jason's eyes
he replies
It's OK, Mom, you had to do
what you had to do

Speak for you! Handsome says in anger
'Cause I'm still looking at this bitch as a stranger.

Jason pushes Handsome and pulls the gun back out
and start repeating, Watch what you saying
I will kill you over my mother and I'm not playing

Jason's mother yells, It's OK for Handsome to be frustrated

Handsome pushes back and they begin fighting
The lamp is broken and now we in darkness
The gun goes off while the front door opens
The other light cuts on to find Pam on the floor, choking
Blood coming out her mouth from the bullet shot
I yell, Oh, my God Jason, what did you do!
He yells back, Don't just blame me
your perfect Handsome was holding the gun too!

Their mother yells, We must call the police!
While crying and holding her, I pronounce she is deceased

To be continued . . .

Acknowledgements

Special thanks:

To God
To my Mother, Karen McIntyre
To my Brother, Charles McIntyre
To all my Family and Friends who had a listening ear
To my Angel

27313159R00090

Made in the USA
Lexington, KY
04 January 2019